The Secret Railway

ELISABETH BERESFORD

The Secret Railway

Illustrated by James Hunt

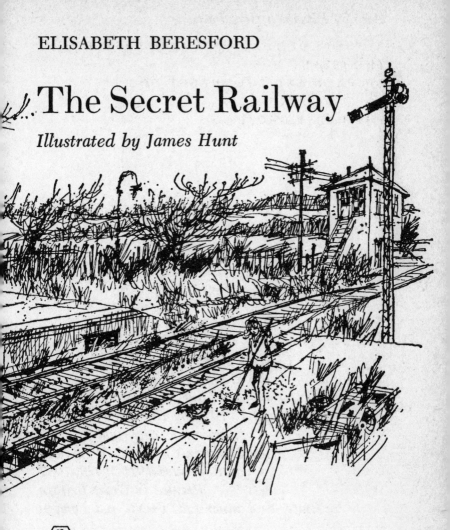

Methuen Children's Books · London

Also by Elisabeth Beresford

KNIGHTS OF THE CARDBOARD CASTLE
THE ISLAND BUS
STEPHEN AND THE SHAGGY DOG
TOBY'S LUCK
THE HAPPY GHOST

First published in Great Britain 1973
by Methuen Children's Books Ltd
11 New Fetter Lane, London EC4P 4EE
Text copyright © 1973 by Elisabeth Beresford
Illustrations copyright © 1973
by Methuen Children's Books Ltd
Reprinted 1975, 1979, 1982
Printed in Great Britain
by Butler & Tanner Ltd, Frome and London

ISBN 0 416 75570 4

Contents

To my technical advisor,
Marcus Robertson.

1 · The secret railway

It was one of those dull, chilly days when the sky looks as if it's been painted grey with too much water put on afterwards so that it's gone all streaky. The sea was a darker grey and even the edges of the waves were off-white as they nibbled at the stony beach and turned the pebbles a shiny brown.

Barny Roberts' feet made a crunching sound as he walked and his shoulders were hunched up round his ears because he was in a bad temper. In fact he'd been in a 'mood', as his mother called it, ever since the Roberts family had moved from Birmingham to Aldport on the Norfolk coast just over three weeks ago.

They had moved because the firm for which Mr Roberts worked, GER Plastics, were hoping to open up a small factory near the little seaside town and it was Mr Roberts' job to get this started.

Barny only understood all this in a hazy kind of

way, but of one thing he was quite sure. He already hated Aldport! It was too small, it was dreadfully dull, there was nothing to do and everybody who lived there seemed to be about ninety years old.

There wasn't even a pier with slot machines on it, just a crumbling stone jetty and a curving harbour wall with a few fishing boats bobbing alongside it.

'Bish!' growled Barny and kicked up a shower of pebbles to try and relieve his feelings. A party of gulls, who had been eyeing him sideways, ruffled up their feathers and opened their beaks as though they were yawning, but didn't bother to move away more than a yard or so.

'There are some ever so pretty shells,' said Sue, Barny's younger sister, who was crouching on her heels and letting the pebbles slide through her fingers.

'Shells!' said Barny with great scorn. 'Who *cares* about silly old *shells*? Oh I wish we were back in Birmingham. There's something to *do* there. There's nothing to do here. Nothing, nothing, NOTHING!'

He waved his arms violently and this time the gulls decided to take notice. They flew up into the grey sky, squawking and wheeling until one by one they landed on the edge of the jetty at a safe distance from this unpleasant noise.

'Well *I* like shells,' said Sue, but she spoke softly, because she knew that when Barny was in a temper it was better to keep quiet. She too missed her home in Birmingham and all her friends and the nice comforting roar and rattle of the traffic, but she knew that Barny minded even more than she did. He'd been the Leader of the Brummie Gang there and they did all kinds of very exciting things, although what kind of things she wasn't too sure except that they did go exploring.

'Shall we explore?' Sue suggested.

'There's nothing *to* explore,' Barny replied, but all the same he came crunching back across the pebbles to the sea-wall where their bicycles were parked.

'You never know,' said Sue, panting along behind him because it is very difficult to walk quickly over a stony beach and her legs were a great deal shorter than his. 'We might find pirates or smugglers or. . . .'

'Not without rocks or cliffs or hidden coves. It's all flat and straight here, *stupid*.' Barny said over his shoulder, 'come on, if you're coming.'

Barny was a very good cyclist. He stood on the pedals without bothering to sit down, so he was soon clear of Aldport, which was wide rather than deep, and out into the marsh land at the back of the town. As the road before him was straight and nearly flat he managed to get up quite a good speed and was almost enjoying the feel of the chilly wind on his face when a despairing cry from behind made him realize that he would have to slow down.

'Now where shall we go?' asked Sue when, very pink in the cheeks, she at last caught up with her brother.

'There's nowhere to go but on this road.'

Barny was perfectly correct for there were no turnings off to left or right, only very flat fields and a windbreak hedge to one side which appeared to follow the line set by the road. There wasn't any traffic either, so Barny began to swoop from side to side until quite suddenly he spotted a track over to his right and on the spur of the moment he decided to take it.

It was quite short, but it went through a break in the hedge at this point and then turned sharp left. It didn't look particularly interesting, but it was better than nothing so he followed it because at least it was something to explore.

Thump, thump, thump Barny's bicycle went, for the path was very rutted and he could hear his cycle bag on the back jumping about, and the bottle of fizzy lemonade in it was obviously rolling all over the place.

'I hope it explodes,' Barny muttered to himself, 'I wish I was back in Birmingham with the Gang. I *hate* Aldport and . . . oh!'

The skidding grass under his wheels suddenly vanished because, out of temper, he had forgotten to watch where he was going and instead of the grass he saw a metal rail and then some rather over-grown wooden sleepers. Barny put on his brakes, but it was too late and he had to fall sideways to stop himself going over the handlebars. A moment later he found that he was lying underneath his bike with the spinning front wheel just above his head.

'Bish!' said Barny shakily and slowly and care-fully got to his feet just as Sue bumped up behind him and asked:

'Are you all right?'

'Course I am.'

'And is your bike?'

'Think so.'

They both began to examine the slightly battered bicycle on which the brake-blocks had become a little twisted so that they hissed against the wheel.

'It's all the fault of this silly path,' Barny said crossly as he levered the blocks back into position. 'It was quite straight and then. . . .'

'Shhh.'

'And then it ran into some silly old railway line. What are you hushing for?'

'Listen!'

It was extremely quiet apart from a few bird noises and the sighing of the wind, but as well as these Sue's sharp ears had noticed quite a different sound. A kind of 'shhh-puff-shhh-puff'.

'We are on a railway line and a train's coming,' Sue whispered.

'Don't be stupid. It's not anything like a diesel or an electric. . . .'

'No, it's not, but it *is*. Oh shhh!'

'Shhh-puff-shhh-puff. . . .'

The strange noise grew louder and Barny found himself staring down the overgrown track. Of course, long, long ago this must have been a proper railway line, but none of the trains he'd ever heard in New Street Station had made a noise like this!

'Bish,' Barny growled and stopped his cycle wheel spinning so that even that soft whirring sound was stilled. He found himself holding his breath, almost as though he expected a phantom train to appear round the curve, but all that came into sight was a red-headed boy.

His bent arms were held in tightly to his sides and moving backwards and forwards like pistons. He was looking straight ahead and he was saying, 'Shhh-puff-shhh-puff. . . .'

He was quite a young boy, bigger than Sue, but not as large as Barny and like them he was wearing a zip-up jacket and jeans. He didn't appear to notice either of them as he drew up alongside, his arms slowing and then coming to a standstill. He let out a final shhhhhhhh. . . .

'Playing at trains are you?' asked Barny in such a rude kind of way that Sue's cheeks turned even more pink.

The boy didn't bother to reply. He suddenly opened his mouth, let out a piercing shriek—which made Barny jump back in alarm—and then slowly at first, but with gathering speed began to move his arms again while at the same time he shuffled backwards.

'Sh-sh-sh-sh-shhhhh. Sh-sh-sh-sh-shhhhh. . . .'

And before either of the Roberts had got over their surprise at this strange meeting, the boy had

13

vanished round the slight curve in the track and all they could hear was a slowly diminishing shhhh. . . .

'He does it jolly well, doesn't he?' said Sue.

'Silly kids' game,' replied Barny, 'pretending to be some sort of a train. It's what *little* children do.'

All the same that sudden shriek had startled him, so just to show that it hadn't really done any such thing, Barny picked up his bike and began to trundle it after the boy, muttering to himself as he went. Sue rattled along behind and once round the curve the pair of them almost collided as they stopped and stared at the scene before them.

Here the track split into two and ran between two high platforms. Platforms over which moss, flowers, weeds and grass had spread so that they almost looked like natural banks. On the righthand platform was one small building about the size of a garden shed. It had four walls, a door and a roof and appeared to be on the point of collapse.

But the building on the lefthand platform was both much larger and a great deal more imposing— or had been once. It was sturdily built and had a roof jutting out to the front which was supported by four pillars.

Underneath this extra roof was a long wooden bench and once, long ago, travellers must have sat

14

there, sheltered from rain and snow during the winter and shadowed from the sun during the summer. But now the roof was full of holes and part of the ornamental woodwork round its edge had come loose and it rattled slightly in the chilly wind.

This building also had two windows—both cracked and dirty—and a couple of doors, one of which was slightly ajar while the other was fully open. A very rusty, unusual looking slot machine stood between the doorways.

The whole station looked not just deserted, but as though it had been empty for years and years. It seemed so sad and forgotten that it made Sue think of the overgrown, cobwebbed castle in The Sleeping Beauty.

'Hi!' shouted Barny, more to break the silence than because he expected the boy to answer. There was no reply and Sue said in a whisper, 'He could be hiding anywhere. Look, there's a great big shed over there on the left. I can see the top of it behind the little hut place.'

'Or he could be up there,' Barny replied, pointing to a signal-box further up the line on the right. He was surprised to find that he was whispering too, so he cleared his throat noisily and plodded on along the line and up the gentle slope of the lefthand platform.

'Hi?' Barny shouted again and then for the second time in a few minutes he nearly jumped out of his skin. There was a furious cackling sound and through the open doorway beside him appeared a very cross looking hen.

'Tck-tck-tck-tck. . . .' she gabbled, pecked at Barny's feet and then scuttled off down the platform, ducked under the tumbledown fence and was lost to sight.

'I'm not scared,' said Barny, who was, and he leant his bike against the wall and walked boldly into the shadowy darkness.

He found himself in a small room which was furnished with a long, leather-covered seat with bits of stuffing bulging out of it, a tiny rusty stove and a very speckled mirror which made his face look green and spotty. There were several piles of extremely dusty papers heaped against the walls and reposing on top of one of the piles was a brown egg.

Sue, who was hovering uncertainly in the doorway, suddenly became aware of approaching footsteps. She turned guiltily to find the strange

boy coming towards her with a stern expression on his face.

'Now then, now then,' he said, 'has the young gentleman gone in there?'

'What young . . . oh you mean my brother! Yes he has, but he won't do any harm.'

'I dare say he won't, but can't he read?'

And the boy pointed to the faint lettering on the window which read:

LADIES WAITING ROOM.

'Oh it's you,' said Barny coming out into the open and with the warm egg in his hand. 'What a funny sort of a. . . .'

'Excuse me, sir,' the boy interrupted politely but firmly, 'but that room is for the use of ladies only. And that's my egg.'

'*I* found it. Now look here. . . .'

'Laid by *my* hen. Thank you sir.'

And the egg was removed from Barny's hold before he could argue any further. The boy slid it gently into his jacket pocket and at the same time produced a large pair of clippers from his belt as he went on, 'Tickets please.'

He did it with such an official voice that Sue and Barny found themselves reaching into their own pockets. Sue produced a crumpled up shopping list and the boy smoothed it out, read it carefully and then clipped a hole in one corner before returning it with a polite, 'Thank you miss.' He then stared sternly at Barny, his hand held out.

'Kids' games,' said Barny in a lordly way.

'Well I think it's a jolly good game and I want to go on playing it,' Sue replied and turning to the boy she asked, 'Is this your own railway station?'

'Travelling without a ticket's an offence you know. No, it isn't. It isn't anybody's station now so I come here quite a bit. Do you like trains?'

'I don't know any,' Sue said regretfully.

'I do. I've got a. . . .' the boy said and then stopped as though he had changed his mind about something. He looked doubtfully at Barny who was whistling between his teeth and gazing down the track as though he wasn't the least interested in their conversation.

'Got a what?' Sue asked.

'Never mind. Look here, if you like *you* can come and work here too. It's not much fun on my own and I can't manage the signals and the points and everything all at once.'

'You mean you can get up into the signal-box and really make things work?' Barny asked.

'Yup. I *can*, she *could*, but you. . . .'

19

The two boys eyed each other in a way which made Sue think of a couple of dogs who aren't sure whether they're going to have a fight or make friends. She held her breath for a moment, listening to the creaking woodwork and the hen clucking busily to herself and their own breathing.

It was all so quiet when once upon a time it must have been full of all kinds of noises—doors being banged shut, the guard's whistle, people calling out 'Goodbye, goodbye. . . .' and bustling about in that anxious way they always did on railway stations, and, louder than everything else put together, the rumbling clatter of the train itself.

It was so difficult to imagine that Sue shut her eyes and screwed up her face with the effort. The wind blew through a hole in the roof with a shrill piping cry and it was as though a ghostly train whistle was sounding miles away across the marshes. As she heard it Sue got the Idea.

'Oh, listen, listen,' she said, 'couldn't we all work the signals and things, the three of us? Couldn't we turn this back into a real station? A proper, real, railway? Couldn't we?'

The boys stopped staring at each other and stared at her instead.

'She doesn't really understand these sort of

20

things,' Barny said, but his voice had stopped being cross for the first time in over three weeks. 'But perhaps it is a sort of an idea. I mean not just playing at railways, but getting stuff working properly. I bet those points are jolly rusted up for a start. Well, what do you think? It's your station really because you were here first.'

It was Barny's way of apologizing for being so squashing earlier without actually saying he was sorry. The boy seemed to understand, because he only hesitated for a moment longer and then he nodded.

'Rusty? I can't budge 'em half the time. We'd better talk it over and make some plans. Come into my office.'

And he led the way down the platform and through the second doorway with Barny at his heels and Sue following on behind chanting to herself:

'We've *got* a *rail*way. Our *own* secret *rail*way. We've got a *rail*way. . . .'

2 · Andy

Andy Fletcher, the red-headed boy, took the egg out of his pocket and placed it carefully in a flower-pot and then nodded to the Roberts to sit down on a battered packing-case while he perched himself on a high stool. He didn't say anything, but let them take their time to look round their surroundings. They were certainly worth looking *at* for it was a most unusual and interesting little room.

Behind Andy's stool was a long wooden shelf which had once been polished and which had a long narrow drawer beneath it, and at the back of this was a narrow window with ECIFFO GNIKOOB stencilled on it with the letters back to front. In the wall facing these strange words was a chimney piece with a rusty black metal object which was a hod for carrying coal.

On the lefthand wall there was a much larger window with iron bars across it and which overlooked what must have once been the station yard.

Along the fourth wall was a row of wooden pegs on which hung a duffle coat, several cloths, a battered broom with its head suspended between two of the hooks, a thick wad of rough paper with string threaded through holes in one corner and finally two railway flags, tidily furled and lassoed by nooses of twine. Beneath this array were four somewhat rusty red lamps of the kind that sometimes mark the spot where there are holes in the road.

In spite of the fact that there were a few tell-tale signs that the hen had visited this part of the station quite recently, the room had a very trim appearance that reminded Barny of his father's office at the factory.

'Well?' said Andy at last.

'Not bad,' replied Barny.

'It's lovely,' said Sue, 'but what does ECIFFO GNIKOOB mean?'

'It's BOOKING OFFICE spelt backwards, stupid,' Barny said quickly. It had been puzzling him too. In fact he had only just worked it out and wanted to show how clever he was.

'It's MY office now,' said Andy, 'well sort of anyway. Hold on, it's getting a bit dark in here.'

He slithered off his stool and went over to one of the red lamps and fiddled with it and then lit it very carefully. It purred softly to itself and a warm, yellow glow spread through the room and made it seem even more friendly.

'Doesn't anybody mind you being here?' asked Sue.

'There's nobody *to* mind,' Andy put the lamp on the shelf and then opened the drawer and took out a pencil and some paper. 'Nobody's been here for years and years except my Great Uncle Fletcher— he was the Station Master here at Marsh End once upon a time when it was the Great Eastern Railway—and he doesn't come any more because it makes him furious.'

'Why?' Barny and Sue asked together.

'Because it does, that's why. Well then, you go on about your idea. What are your names, anyway?'

Everybody exchanged names. Barny had been thinking very fast but he wasn't at all sure that he knew quite *what* they wanted to do exactly. He was rather vague about railways, except that it was rather fun travelling very fast on a train and outpacing cars on a motorway. Finally he said, 'First of all, tell us about this place.'

'Well I dunno,' said Andy, shifting about on his high stool.

'Go on,' said Sue encouragingly, 'I like stories, it's better than television. Go on.'

'Well,' Andy took a deep breath. 'If you want to go back to the start, it's like this, eh? A long time ago, well about a hundred years or so, more or less, there was this man called Stephenson who invented, sort of, railway engines. Steam engines. . . .'

'He did it more'n a hundred years ago,' interrupted Barny. 'We learnt about him in school. And it was about the 1830s, I think. . . .' he added uncertainly.

'Who's telling, you or me?'

'You,' said Sue, 'anyway dates don't matter all that much. Go on.'

'Well he did anyway, invent steam engines that is. And people got ever so excited and angry too because they said that the noise of the engines and the speed and all that'd drive everybody mad and the animals as well. But Queen Victoria, she took a ride and. . . .'

'We learnt about her in school,' said Sue.

'Shut up,' put in Barny. 'Go on.'

'And her husband, who was called Prince Albert, he got in a right stew because when they stopped he went up to the front of the train and said "Not so fast Mister Engine Driver, please" and they'd only been doing about twenty miles an hour so my Great Uncle Fletcher says, although he wasn't there of course.

'Well then,' Andy took another deep breath, 'after a while like, everybody saw as railways'd be the best way—the fastest way—to travel so all kinds of companies started up building engines and tracks and stations. There weren't any cars or good roads in those days, eh? And one of the lines they built came through here, Marsh End, to Aldport and. . . .'

'Why?' asked Barny.

"Cause in those days Aldport was an important place what with the fishing and the harbour and people coming on their holidays. There was trains —steam trains—up and down the line all the time. My Great Uncle Fletcher, he can recall when the Royalty came here.'

'Queen Victoria?' asked Sue, her eyes round and shining in the gathering dusk.

'Not her, no, but later on, her grandchildren going to Sandringham which is up in Norfolk, but they were Royalty just the same and my Great Uncle Fletcher used to wear his top hat and a funny black coat. He's still got 'em.'

'Then what happened?' demanded Barny.

'Well some lines were electrified and some weren't and some turned to diesel and some were just closed down. Nearly everybody's got cars now, you see, and lines like this got more and more poor until they'd got no money left so they were closed down. Like this 'un.'

'What a sad story,' said Sue after a very long pause.

'But it's still *here*,' said Barny, 'even if there aren't any more trains. I've never seen a steam engine.'

There was another long silence and then Andy said in a very off-hand voice:

'Would you like to?'

'I wouldn't mind.'

'Come on then.'

Andy picked up the purring lantern and jerked his head. It was growing quite dusky and dark by this time and Sue and Barny were almost treading on his heels as he led the way out of the Booking Office and down the overgrown platform and then across the weedy line to the other side of the double track which ran through the station. Sue caught a glimpse of something small and shadowy bouncing away from the glow of the lantern and she gave a 'yiiip' and grabbed at Barny.

'It's only a rabbit,' said Andy, 'there's plenty of them round this place, eh?'

'I've never seen a rabbit before,' said Sue, straining her eyes after the bobbing white patch which was the rabbit's tail. 'I thought they were all dead.'

'Not them,' said Andy, 'place is full of 'em. You wait till you see the hares. March is the time for hares.'

'Are they dangerous?' Sue whispered.

'No.' Andy laughed in the gathering gloom. 'They won't do you no harm, it's the corn they're after, 'sides which in March they just go round and round and round. My Great Uncle Fletcher he says they're one of the fastest animals there are, only they run in circles, see?'

'March hares,' exclaimed Barny, stopping so suddenly that Sue bumped into him. 'I never thought of that before. Mad as a March hare, that's what people say about other people. Are they really mad? The hares, I mean?'

'Only in March,' said Andy firmly, although he wasn't at all sure about this point himself. 'Come along do or it'll be too dark to see anything. This is a secret, mind . . . swear you won't tell nobody?'

'Cross my heart and spit on the ceiling—well the sky,' said Barny, 'but only if—oh I say!'

Andy had led them across the main tracks until they were facing the booking office and had unbolted the very rusty locks of a large shed—the same shed that Sue had caught sight of earlier—to disclose a large, *very* large, dark bulk which rose above them and almost touched the shadowy roof.

Sue tipped back on her heels and gazed upwards, her eyes as round as buttons. Even Barny, who had been telling himself all along that he was not going to be impressed by anything that Andy should disclose, was stunned into silence.

Above the purring yellow light of the lantern rose an imposing shape. It was black and rusted and rather dusty and yet at the same time neither age nor decay had managed to detract from its dignity and power. It was still and silent now, but a great force and strength still lived inside it and Barny, who had often seen the giant machines at the GER works pounding away about their business, said quietly, 'It's—it's a smasher, super. . . .'

'It's a 4–6–OT,' said Andy. 'It was left here in 1966 . . . it's a grand engine, eh?'

'It is that.'

They walked round it slowly, their hands stroking

the dusty, rusty sides while Sue trailed after them looking up at the funnel. She had never seen an engine like this before and she had never had any idea that they were so big. Somehow when you were standing on a platform at a railway station trains, although noisy and important, hadn't seemed quite so large.

'Why is the engine here?' asked Barny looking at Andy in the yellow glow.

'I don't know all of it. The line was closed down and she was—that is, this engine was shunted into this shed and left. She's been here ever since. Nobody seems to care, except my Great Uncle Fletcher and me, and he doesn't care no more either. She's called the Great Eastern Queen if you're interested and she's not bad, eh?'

'She's all right,' said Barny, 'not bad at all really. But what'll happen to her?'

'Dunno.'

'Does she still go?' asked Sue, who had been wondering how the train driver had ever managed to climb up into his cab as it was so far off the ground. In the dull light she was unable to see the special steps up the side.

'Probably would,' replied Andy shortly. He was already regretting that he had taken anybody to visit the most important thing in his life. 'Come on, you're best out of here, there'll be bats and that. Remember now, you swore you wouldn't tell nobody. If They know she's here they might take her away for scrap.'

'Who is "they"?' Barny asked as Andy bolted up the shed door.

'I dunno,' Andy growled. 'They, Them . . . it's getting night time, you'd best be off back to your home.'

'Can we come back again?' Sue asked timidly. 'It's ever so dull where we are and it would be fun to pretend—well, to try and run our own railway with the points and signals and everything, wouldn't it Barny?'

Andy held the oil lantern up and he and Barny looked at each other in the soft yellow glow.

'It'd be rather fun,' said Barny, 'better than dull old Aldport anyway.'

'It's got to be run proper,' said Andy, 'and there's a lot of things that'll be needed.'

'I know. Oil and rags and probably a screwdriver and a spade. . . .'

'And dusters and a broom, a *proper* broom, and curtains and cushions. . . .' said Sue.

'And a drip can. . . .'

'And polish and cushions and curtains. . . .' Sue repeated.

Both boys stopped talking and stared at her and then Andy said with dreadful scorn.

'*Cushions*! *Curtains*! This is a *railway station* not a doll's house.'

'Sorry,' said Sue meekly. Luckily for her Barny was too busy with his own list to take much notice, otherwise he might have been a bit suspicious at the way in which Sue didn't argue.

It wasn't until they were getting on their bikes that Andy rather punctured the air of excitement by saying suddenly, 'Oil and a spade and a screwdriver'll cost money and I haven't got any.'

'No pocket money?' asked Barny.

'No.' Andy turned down the wick in the lantern and the light died with a plopping sound. In the dusk the Roberts couldn't see the way in which Andy's face had turned red under its orange freckles. He went on stolidly, 'My Dad's an agricultural labourer and the pay's not grand. So I have to work if I want money, only there's not much work for boys round here in the holidays, 'cause the older boys get first chance, eh?'

There was an awkward pause and then Barny

33

c

said, 'Oh well, we'll worry about that later. I've got some pocket money saved up. OK?'

Just for a moment Andy felt a horrid, bitter taste in his mouth. It was *his* railway, his station, his train—at least it had been—and now he'd let two strangers into his secret, two strangers with the money with which to buy all the things Marsh End needed to get straight and smart again. But perhaps the more important part of the bargain was the railway itself.

'OK,' Andy said slowly, 'but we will sort it out later. See you tomorrow then 'bout eleven? You'd best bring some sandwiches.'

'See you,' Barny agreed and Sue echoed her brother.

Andy watched them ride away, the light from their rear-lamps bumping up and down. He made certain again that he had shut everything up securely and as the bats, fast as black lightning, flickered round the roof he called out, 'Ellie, Ellie, Ellie. . . .'

There was a squawk and a scuffle and the hen came slithering under the fence and pecked at his boots.

'Where've you been laying now then?' demanded Andy. 'Come on, it's time we went home.' He cradled the flower-pot with the egg in it under his arm and set off across the fields to the cottage where he lived with Ellie flapping at his heels.

Andy had a lot on his mind, particularly the knotty problem of getting the points unstuck, otherwise he might have taken notice of two things. The first was that the curtain in his Great Uncle's cottage twitched as he went past and there was a perfectly furious honking from the front garden. The second was a very battered, brightly painted van with the words FLETCHER GROUP which was travelling far too fast down the straight marsh road towards Aldport.

3 · Getting up steam

Mrs Roberts said for the fourth time at breakfast on the following morning, 'But who *is* this Andy Fletcher and why does he want to borrow a spade and an oilcan and where are you going to meet him and what is he *like*?'

'He's all right,' said Barny, also for the fourth time, 'and he wants the spade for digging.'

'He's very nice and he's got red hair and a hen,' said Sue.

'A *hen*!' exclaimed Mrs Roberts.

'Yes, and it lays eggs all over the—the—the place,' replied Sue, her voice getting faster and faster, 'lovely big brown eggs with speckles in the shells and. . . .'

'Dear me,' Mrs Roberts stopped looking worried and she also stopped making the sandwiches, which made Barny anxious as he was always hungry, even after a good meal. 'Dear me, I haven't seen eggs like that since I was your age and your grandad used to bring them home sometimes from the country. They were lovely eggs those were, I've never forgotten the taste ... but you still haven't said *where* you're going!'

Barny and Sue exchanged a look of silent desperation and then Barny said quickly, 'Marsh End, you must have heard of it, Mum, it's quite close to here. I say, eight sandwiches isn't very much.'

'I'd rather keep *you* a week than a fortnight,' said Mrs Roberts. 'All right then, but mind you bring that spade and the can back safe now, or your Dad'll go mad.'

'I'll tell *you* something,' said Sue somewhat breathlessly as forty minutes later they cycled side by side out of Aldport, the breathlessness being caused by the number of assorted objects that they were carrying strapped to their racks, 'and that is, it's the first time I've heard Mum being funny since we came here. You're not the only one who's been cross, she has too. *And* Dad. . . .'

'I dunno what you're on about,' replied Barny not quite truthfully. He had been so bundled up in his own miseries about leaving Birmingham and the Gang that he hadn't thought much about anything else, although now he came to consider it Mum and Dad hadn't been like they used to be. Dad, who had always been OK about lending his tools at home, had been quite dodgy this morning. It was all very unsettling so Barny only growled again, 'I dunno, come on or we won't get there by eleven.'

Andy, Ellie clucking round his gumboots, was waiting for them impatiently.

'Come on, come on,' he said, 'I say, what you got there, eh?'

Sue wisely kept her mouth shut and did not disclose that she had brought on the back of her bike a bundle of old cushions, her mother's best scissors, a tin of half-used furniture polish, two lengths of material which had once been intended for curtains that had never been made, and the sewing kit that she had used in the Brownies.

'I've got a spade, an oilcan and a torch and a notebook and biro,' replied Barny, 'and I borrowed all of 'em, OK?'

'OK,' agreed Andy and grinned right across his freckled face. 'Now I've been thinking and I think the first thing is the points because they don't work properly at all, eh?'

'Let's have a look, eh?' said Barny.

The wind was still tearing bitterly across the marsh, but there wasn't a cloud in the sky which was a bright pale blue. A skein of geese arrowed their way across it, but everybody at Marsh End was too busy to notice them.

Andy had drawn a rough map of the station and the two boys crouched over it on the platform. In the full light of day it was far more complicated and interesting than Barny had thought it would be.

'Why does it turn into two lines going through the station?' he asked.

'Has to, doesn't it, eh? Look, you've got a train coming due east from Marsh Junction, that is—or used to be 'cause it's gone now—although it's still there though not used—ten miles from here. Then you've got a train going due west from Aldport, so the two of 'em'll pass. Well, where will they do it or take on their passengers if not from here? See?'

'Hang about a bit,' Barny said, his head starting to swim. 'Yes, OK, but how does each train get on the right lines? I mean they could run into each other!'

'Oh deary me,' said Andy, 'trains are like cars— or cars are like trains come to that, as trains was here first—so they pass on the left. Now look, it's quite straightforward. Signal Box A, on the map here passes the message down the line to Signal Box B that the train from Marsh Junction is coming through Marsh End and so they alters the points to let her through. . . .'

'Hold on.' said Barny. '*How*?'

Andy took a deep breath and started all over again. To him it was quite straightforward and simple because ever since he was small his Great Uncle Fletcher had been explaining the whole fascinating way in which the railways worked, but then you had to make allowances for people from big cities who didn't know about these things.

Meanwhile Sue was doing her own exploring and had discovered that just outside the shed where the great steam engine lived was a railway coach. Its

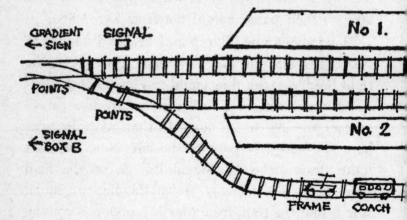

MARSH END STATION (DRAWN BY A. FLETCHER)

windows were unbroken and although it was very high off the rails she managed to open one of the doors and to scramble up and into it.

The carriage was very dusty and dirty and it smelt somehow unused, but it was also a good deal warmer and less draughty than the booking office and there were, of course, a great many comfortable seats. Sue plumped down on one of them and then sneezed violently as a cloud of dust flew up around her. She half shut her eyes and bounced up and down, pretending that she was travelling very fast through a foreign country.

In the distance she could hear the boys both

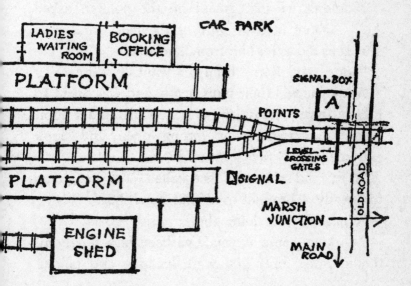

talking at once, the clinking noise made by the spade against the rails and then a very rusty, clanking sound followed by cries of triumph.

'Undone one of their old points I suppose,' said Sue to herself, 'well I'd better get on if I want to surprise them and there's a lot to be done.'

Within a very few minutes the dust was swirling out of the carriage and Ellie who had come hopping over the lines to investigate, retreated hurriedly with an angry 'tck-tck-tck-TCK'.

It was nearly two hours after this that Barny could resist the truly awful pangs of hunger no longer and called a halt for food.

'Couldn't we just grease up the points?' asked Andy, whose face in spite of the cold wind, was almost as red as his hair from hard work.

'Nope,' said Barny firmly. 'I want my dinner!'

Andy stacked their tools neatly and was about to follow Barny across the line towards the station when a carriage door swung open and Sue's extremely dusty face appeared.

'Your food's in here,' she called. 'I've got yours too, Andy. I brought over your lunch box.'

'What are you doing there?' Andy asked.

'Working, same as you. I've been here nearly all the morning, only you were banging and talking such a lot you didn't notice. I walked right past you twice. Oh come *on*,' Sue swung out even further in her impatience, 'I want you to see what I've done.'

She had done a great deal and the boys were generous enough to say so for the carriage, although still shabby, was now dirt and dust free and smelt pleasantly of polish.

'Cor—smashing,' said Andy.

'Not half bad,' agreed Barny, 'and *you've* got a moustache.'

Sue ignored this remark and flipping a very dirty cloth over her arm she said:

'First dinner is now being served in the restaurant car, this way please gentlemen,' and led the way to the section of the coach where she had put up the folding table, which was attached to one side of the carriage, and had laid out on it all their picnic things.

Everybody ate without bothering to talk until there wasn't a single crumb or even an apple core left and then Barny rapped on the table with his knuckles and said loudly, 'I've been thinking and I think this, we should form ourselves into a Board of Directors and. . . .'

'What's that?' asked Andy.

'Why?' asked Sue.

'If you'd both kindly shut up, I'll tell you. Because firms always have Boards of Directors, at least they do at GER where Dad works, and they're the people who say how the firm is to run, what work's to be done and that sort of thing.'

'But there's only us,' said Sue, 'and Ellie, but you can't count her really because of her being a hen.'

'Yes you can,' contradicted Andy, 'because we can have some of her eggs if you like and that'd make her like part of the restaurant car.'

'I say, could we?' Sue asked, 'I told Mum about Ellie's eggs and she was ever so interested. I SAY!' And she put her hands over her ears and made a terrible face.

'Shut up,' ordered Barny, rapping very loudly and then adding 'ouch' because he'd grazed his knuckles earlier on the points, 'order, order.'

'I can't,' Sue replied, 'I'm having an Idea. Yes, that's it. Listen Andy, you could sell Ellie's eggs to Mum, yes you *could*,' she added hastily as Andy opened his mouth to argue, 'because she has to buy them anyway at the Supermarket and they're not nearly as large as Ellie's are and I know Mum'd rather have the brown speckled ones. Then with that money we could, *you* could, buy any other sort of things we might need. There!'

There was a pause during which Barny generously kept quiet although he was longing to put his own plan to the company, and Andy chewed on his lower lip and thought the idea over.

'OK,' he said at last, 'it's a deal. Shake hands on it.'

'Now then,' said Barny, when this had been done, 'now then, what about MY idea? Didn't the railways used to have Boards of Directors once upon a time?'

'Yes,' Andy nodded, 'so my Great Uncle Fletcher says, but it was a long, long time ago and what's the good of it, eh?'

'It means we can run this railway the way *we* want to,' Barny replied, 'with nobody else interfering in it. We'll have to vote on things too. If two people say yes to an idea and one person says no, then the two people win and the third person has to give in. And we can get out a proper plan of what we want to do. Do you agree? If you do, put up your hands.'

After another pause two hands were duly raised and Barny wrote on his note pad:

'The Marsh End Railway Company. Directors: A. Fletcher. B. Roberts. S. Roberts. Future Plans: 1'

He read this out and Andy said at once, 'To free, oil and get in working order the points as they are very covered in weeds. Agreed?'

'Agreed,' said Barny, writing as fast as he could. 'Go on, Sue.'

'I'd much rather do the curtains. . . .'

'Well you can't, you're out-voted.'

However, in a very short space of time Sue discovered that the boys were quite capable of dealing with their plans without any help from her so she slipped back to the coach to continue with her own work.

The minutes hurried past without anybody noticing as they were so busy and dusk was settling over the Marsh by the time that Andy called a halt. The points had now all been cleared of weeds and earth and were working remarkably smoothly, while the coach had gained several cushions and some curtains so that it had a very cosy air about it when the Board of Directors made an appointment to meet the following day.

'What's *that*?' asked Barny as they paused in the dusk just short of the main platform and he pointed to a gaunt trolley on wheels which stood on the track.

'It's a frame, isn't it?' Andy replied. 'Look I'll show you.'

And he jumped on to the flat looking object and tugged at a lever. There was a protesting screech and the thing moved a few inches towards the points.

'Hold on,' Barny shouted and nipped across and pulled the points, 'Go on. . . .'

Andy heaved at the lever and the frame, which resembled a railway truck without any sides to it, lumbered forwards, paused momentarily at the points and then clanked towards the two main lines.

'Can't do no more,' said Andy, his lungs going like bellows. 'It's too rusty, eh?'

'But . . .' Barny danced from foot to foot in the half light, 'it goes!'

"Course it does,' Andy replied, sliding down from his perch, 'but it isn't half hard work. Don't suppose it's been moved for years. Why?'

'Don't you see!' Barny shouted, 'we could ride on it, like a real train. We could set the signals and the points and it'd be "our" train, eh?'

'Um, we'll see in the morning,' Andy replied after thinking this over, 'you'd best get back home.'

Neither Barny nor Sue understood the principle on which the frame worked, but the idea of having

47

their own train on which they could ride was so interesting that they could hardly wait to get back to Marsh End the next day. That evening when they were both in bed asleep Mrs Roberts said to her husband:

'I suppose it's all right the pair of them going off like this when we don't know anything about this new friend of theirs. Still, I must say Barny looks a lot happier than he did. How are things going at the works, Ted?'

'I dunno,' Mr Roberts shook his head. 'The firm could open up a factory here all right, it's a nice enough place even if it is quiet, and there's enough people around needing jobs. The trouble is that they all live so far apart and most of 'em have only got bikes.'

He smiled ruefully. 'You can't expect a man to cycle fifteen miles to work in the morning and then home again at night, specially during the winter months. Then there's the freight problem to be reckoned with. The lanes and roads hereabouts just weren't built for heavy traffic. Yes—transport will be the difficulty and that's what I'll have to tell Mr Denton, the Area Manager, when he comes down to see us. Seems a shame though.'

'Why?'

'Well they need the work round here. Since Aldport isn't a big fishing port any more and there aren't that many holiday visitors, things are pretty hard and I gather that some of the local lads are starting to get troublesome. I dunno what the answer is and that's a fact.'

'Do you like the place, Ted?' Mrs Roberts asked.

'It's not bad. A bit quieter than Birmingham though. Did Barny bring back my spade?'

'He did.' Mrs Roberts put down her darning and looked at her husband, 'And do you know what, Ted, he'd cleaned it up a treat! It looks as good as new. Now what do you make of *that*?'

'I dunno. But maybe this Fletcher boy is a good kind of friend for Barny to have. A boy who knows how to take care of tools must be all right. Now stop worrying, Barny and Sue won't get into any trouble in a quiet sort of place like this.'

A mere twelve hours later Barny and Sue were just discovering what trouble might be, for Andy, having arrived some time ahead of them, had thoroughly cleaned and greased the wheels and lever of the frame as well as having set the points.

'Come on, come on,' he shouted as they rode up on to the platform. 'I've got this working.'

'Steady up,' replied Barny, 'we've got to put it to

the vote you know. All those in favour raise their right hands.'

Nobody voted against the idea, although Sue wasn't at all sure about whether or not she wanted to climb up on to the strange looking platform on wheels. Although it had no engine it seemed both large and powerful.

'All right,' she agreed as Andy pulled and Barny pushed her up on to the frame, 'only where are we going and can we stop it?'

"Course we can,' replied Andy, who had not, in fact, given this problem any thought. 'Barny, you take this side of the handle. Sue, you sit down there. One, two, three and OFF.'

The frame, grumbling and complaining in spite of all the recent oiling, moved forwards slowly with the boys heaving at the lever with all their strength while Sue sat on the dusty side and watched her dangling feet pass over the grassy siding. Ellie, roused by the noise, came squawking across from the main platform and then vanished right in front of the frame. Sue shouted and the boys looked over their shoulders. Ellie suddenly reappeared almost from underneath the great steel wheels. She flapped her wings and with an indignant 'TCK-TCK' landed beside Sue, her feathers all fluffed up.

50

'Points ahead,' Barny yelled.

The frame seemed to hesitate for a moment, there was a grinding sound and then it swayed, shook and rattled, righted itself and moved on to the main line for Aldport. Andy and Barny exchanged triumphant glances and swung the lever down with renewed energy. It really was a remarkable sensation to be under one's own steam, so to speak, and to feel this large piece of machinery obeying one's efforts.

They were so high up they could see over the hedges and across the flat marshy landscape and

Barny said breathlessly, 'I say, this—this is—oooof —smashing. . . .'

'Not bad, oooof—eh?'

'We're going ever so fast,' called out Sue, who now had the anxious Ellie roosting in her lap.

'And it's not nearly such hard work as it was,' Barny replied, still gripping his side of the lever but no longer having to make an effort to control it. 'It's almost going by itself, isn't it, Andy?'

Andy didn't reply. He was staring straight ahead at the railway line which led directly to Aldport. A small, very weatherbeaten wooden kind of signpost beside the track came nearer and nearer and Andy stared at it intently. His Great Uncle Fletcher had told him time and again what that sign meant. It was the gradient sign and on it in faded lettering were the figures '1/100'.

'Oh deary me,' said Andy, 'oh, oh, oh. . . .'

'What is it?' Barny asked.

'We're on the gradient,' Andy replied, 'that means like downhill and that's why we're going so easy. . . .'

'Well it's a lot less work. . . .'

'We got to stop it!' Andy shouted. 'We're running away. We'll go faster and faster and then we'll crash. We got to stop it.'

'How?' Barny yelled.

'I dunno. . . .'

The frame gathered speed, its wheels clanking rhythmically on the rails, the hedges starting to turn into a blur as Andy and Barny stared at each other in growing consternation.

4 · Trouble

It was one thing to set a machine in motion and quite another to try and stop it as the Board of Directors of the newly formed GER Railway Company now discovered very quickly.

The frame, as though thoroughly enjoying its new found freedom after all these months of rusting away on a siding, continued to gather speed as it went 'clickty-click-clickty-click' down the slight gradient. Sue was also enjoying herself and even Ellie had regained her composure and had begun to explore the floorboards for possible grain.

'We've got to stop it,' Barny yelled.

'I know, I know, but how?' Andy replied.

'Let's try and put it in reverse . . . fight the lever.'

Both boys tugged against the movement of the frame with all their strength, although it seemed as though their arms were being jerked out of their shoulder sockets. There was little effect, but Andy remembered vaguely his Great Uncle Fletcher telling him something about frames having brakes on their sides.

There was a rusty looking lever just by his right hand and Andy, with a kind of desperate courage, jammed it down as hard as he could. His whole body seemed to be jarred from stem to stern and he felt himself being thrown forwards so violently that his teeth quite distinctly rattled in his head. There was a dreadful screeching sound and he found himself being thrown up into the pale blue sky. . . .

'Are you all right?' asked a very shaky voice from a long way away.

'No,' replied Andy and shut his eyes again.

'You don't look dead,' said Sue. 'You landed on your shoulders, sort of. So you're all right really, aren't you?'

There was a very long silence and then Andy reluctantly opened his eyes again and looked up at Barny and Sue who were bending over him. He felt a bit sick and rather sore, but apart from that things didn't seem to be too bad so he got up rather shakily and shook his head.

'We stopped,' said Barny, only his teeth were

chattering so it sounded as if he'd said, 'We shh-ttt-opped.'

'Isn't it a pity?' Sue said regretfully. 'We were having such a lovely ride. I nearly fell off and Ellie's ever so cross, aren't you?'

'It was you that stopped us,' Barny said in a low voice. 'If you hadn't've done . . . are you *sure* you're OK?'

'Yes, I think so.'

Andy moved his arms and legs cautiously, but apart from a distinct ache across his shoulder blades everything appeared to be in working order. He didn't feel quite so sick either, which was a great relief. He turned and looked at the frame. *It* seemed all right too, in fact it looked as if it had been stuck on this part of the line all its life. The two boys gazed up at it and then at each other.

'It's not as easy as I thought it'd be, having a ride,' Barny said slowly.

'We've got to learn how things work,' Andy agreed. 'I always thought it'd be simple running a railway, but it isn't. We'd best get it back up the gradient if we can, but it'll be hard work.'

It was and it took them the rest of the morning to do it as the frame, with its great weight behind it plus the pull of the gradient, showed a distinct partiality for sliding backwards. Sue did her bit too and the result was that a somewhat subdued and aching meeting of the Board of Directors was held in the Restaurant Car.

'I tell you what,' said Barny, who had been drawing diagrams on his notepad, 'if we want to use the frame again, we'll have to work out a better braking system. Just shoving a piece of metal on to the rim of the wheels is bound to make trouble.'

'You're telling me,' agreed Andy, rubbing his sore shoulders. 'But what sort of system, eh?'

'I'll think of something,' replied Barny as he frowned ferociously, trying to remember the workings of some of the giant machines that he'd seen in the factory in Birmingham and wishing now he'd paid attention to them. 'All the same we *did* get the points working OK and the line and I vote. . . .'

'I vote,' put in Sue so loudly that both boys looked up in astonishment, 'I vote that we all do something nice and ordinary like cleaning up the platform and the Booking Office. You—we—can't run a railway unless it looks nice and clean. You've cleaned up your old points, so now it's my turn and I vote for what I want, so there.'

As everybody had been rather scared by the runaway tactics of the frame Sue's vote was carried, although somewhat reluctantly, and for the next few days the Directors of the GER weeded, scrubbed, washed and polished until the old railway station once again began to look more its old self.

It was a gradual change and it took a great deal of hard work. Andy nailed up the loose coping over the main platform and whitewashed it with a gallon of whitewash that his father's employer had generously let him have. Barny carried out some repair work on the railings using *his* father's hammer and nails, incidentally hammering his own fingers quite considerably, while Sue scrubbed and polished her way through both the Ladies Waiting Room and the Booking Office.

When they had finished the whole of Marsh End Station had begun to look so spruce and well cared for that the Directors, in spite of being very tired, also felt extremely proud.

'After all,' said Andy, admiring his own particular handiwork in the pale light of the setting sun, 'there's no *hurry* about getting the line working. And I tell you what, it wouldn't be a bad idea to get the inside of the station whitewashed. . . .'

'Or the station placard bits re-painted,' agreed Barny, who was admiring his own hard work and thinking how professional it looked. There was something very satisfying about a line of fencing which was dead straight and smart. Even Ellie wouldn't be able to squeeze her way through those small gaps!

'And p'raps I could mend the stuffing in the Ladies Waiting Room seats,' put in Sue. 'Sticky tape might do it, I suppose. . . . Have you got the eggs for Mum, Andy?'

Andy handed over a flower-pot in which reposed six very large, brown speckled eggs and reluctantly looked away from his re-roofing job.

'Here you are. You're sure the price is OK?'

' 'Course I am. See you tomorrow then?'

'Yeah.'

The three Directors parted unwillingly, the Senior Director going off across the twilit fields with Ellie at his heels and passing once again a small cottage where the curtains twitched and two bright eyes followed his progress without his realizing it.

'Now what are they doing?' said Great Uncle Fletcher, letting the curtain drop. 'What they up to eh? Shut up, Gladys *do*!' This last remark was addressed to a very large white goose which was flapping and honking up and down the garden.

The last Station Master of Marsh End pushed his

hand backwards and forwards across his chin and glowered at the walls of his small parlour. He'd known for the last week or more that something had been going on at the old derelict station, but as he hated seeing it in its present condition he'd kept well away. Once upon a time it had been a real pleasure to the eye, but now it was all overgrown and tumbledown and not a lick of paint or polish on it. Horrible.

Still, all the same, *something* was going on there and it might be as well to keep an eye on things.

The old man got to his feet and then hesitated as he heard raindrops falling against the windows. It wasn't a night on which to go exploring when a man reached his age! It'd be far wiser to go and have a look at the mischief of Marsh End tomorrow.

Great Uncle Fletcher sat down again and turned on his television set—with the volume well up as he was extremely deaf.

However in spite of his age he didn't sleep late in the mornings so by just after eight he was hobbling off down the footpath and into the lane and then across the Aldport Road, only to be brought up short by the sight of the newly whitewashed and repaired railings and the roof. The old place looked almost as smart as it ever had.

His eyes brightened and he moved faster until he reached the Booking Office and pushed open the door. His hearing might not be so good, but there was nothing the matter with his sight and Great Uncle Fletcher stared round the small room with his jaw dropped while his weatherbeaten, wrinkled face turned a deep red so that he strongly resembled an angry turkey cock.

'It's disgusting! It's disgraceful,' he spluttered.

'So *that's* what young Andy's been up to—and at his age! Just wait till I tell his Dad! Just wait, that's all,' and he thumped his stick on the floor.

However after a few minutes, during which he chomped his jaws up and down as though he was eating something, Great Uncle Fletcher muttered, 'No, 'twouldn't be fair to go talking on to Andy's Dad about this. It'd be better to face the lad straight with it. It's those London children as has put him up to it, I shouldn't be surprised. Foreign habits they've got. No, I'll speak direct to the lad. Come here you.'

This last remark was addressed to the packing case on which Barny and Sue had perched on their first morning at the station. Great Uncle Fletcher hooked hold of it with the crook at the end of his stick, dragged it out on to the platform and sat down and glowered across the tracks.

To think that Marsh End should come to *this*! His jaws chomped steadily.

Happily unaware of the unexpected turn of events the Board of Directors of the GER were going about their own affairs. Sue was buying more polish with the money raised from the sale of Ellie's eggs and Barny was asking his father's advice as to how to mend glass.

'You'd need a proper glazier for that, son,' said Mr Roberts, 'that's a man who specializes in mending—here!' He stopped suddenly and looked up from the papers which he had spread across the kitchen table, 'Here, what do you want to know a thing like that for? Have you been *breaking* windows, come on, own up?'

Breaking—why should I *break* windows?' asked Barny in surprise.

Mr Roberts fiddled with a slide-rule and straightened some pencils and then he said slowly, 'Well then, there was a bit of trouble in the middle of the town last night. It seems some lads got out of hand and went round smashing things just for the fun of it. You were out latish and I know you've been bored, that you don't like it here and. . . .'

'Dad!' Barny burst out, 'it wasn't me. I wouldn't do a thing like that and anyway I'm not bored now at all because I'm—I'm. . . . Well anyway, it wasn't me.'

'All right, all right calm down,' Mr Roberts said hastily for Barny was now as red-faced and furious as Great Uncle Fletcher had been a short while ago. 'I didn't really think it was, only you asking about mending glass is a bit unusual. What are you up to exactly, you and Sue?'

'It's—it's nothing bad,' Barny replied and then hesitated as it occurred to him first that they might be trespassing at Marsh End and secondly he suddenly recalled with awful clarity the near disaster of the runaway frame. 'It's nothing that sort of bad,' he finished lamely.

'Can't you tell me?'

'Not exactly. It's kind of like a game that we're playing and it's smashing fun. When it's all ready like, I *will* tell you and Mum, only we have to take a vote on it, because it's not just me that's in it. See?'

'I think so,' said Mr Roberts, who by now was feeling distinctly muddled. He took a deep breath and looked up, 'I know you don't like it very much here, Barny, and I agree it *is* quiet after Birmingham, although . . . well, what I'm trying to say is, how'd you feel about going back there? You'd be glad wouldn't you?'

Barny opened his mouth to say 'yes' and then shut it again and frowned. A couple of weeks ago he'd have been overjoyed at the idea, because then he'd hated being stuck in Aldport which had seemed to be just about the dullest place in the whole world. Only now, somehow, it was all a bit different because there was the Station and the

Secret Railway and a great deal of hard work still to be done.

Why, they hadn't even tackled the signal-box or the level crossing and Andy had promised to explain to him how to work the signals marked A and B on the plan, which showed that the line was either busy or clear. What's more, they hadn't begun to tackle the problem of the Marsh Junction points, and. . . .

'I dunno,' said Barny uncertainly. 'I mean yes, I suppose it'd be all right to go back to Brum. Why Dad?'

'Well things aren't going too well here, son; look at this map. Now then, the firm's thinking of building an oil rig off the coast at this point,' and Mr Roberts drew a circle with his pencil, 'well, as you know, oil equals hydro-carbons and those can equal polythene, which is one of our products. You follow me?'

'Um,' said Barny, nodding wisely.

'Yes, well, which means that the firm'd be more than willing to build a factory near Aldport. There's plenty of labour round about because. . . .'

'There's more men wanting jobs than there are jobs going,' agreed Barny, who had absorbed this information from Andy.

65

'That's right,' said Mr Roberts, 'but travelling into Aldport's the problem. The labour force, that's the men who need the work, are spread over a very large area. Some of 'em have bikes, some have cars or vans and then again some of 'em haven't got any form of transport and, of course, it's the same for the women. Then there's the problem of transporting freight too. It's all very difficult I can tell you.'

Barny forgot his own pressing affairs as he studied the map. His father had never talked to him quite like this before, treating him as though he were grown-up, and it made him feel both important and rather worried, because this was a new sort of world in which real people with families were involved.

'I dunno,' said Barny.

'And neither do I,' agreed Mr Roberts, rolling up his papers. 'It'll be up to my boss, Mr Denton, to make the final decision—well, go on, off with you son, only don't get up to any mischief mind and if you want to find out about a glazier you'd do well to ask down at the Post Office. The woman that works there seems to know everybody *and* their business, and Barny?'

'Yes Dad?'

'I'd like to know what you and Sue are up to— when you've voted on it.'

'Yes Dad.'

Half an hour later Sue had returned with the polish and Barny had discovered from the woman at the Post Office that her nephew was first rate at mending glass (only he was very busy at the moment what with the trouble down in the town centre last night). They were cycling along the marsh road towards the station when Sue said, 'I'll tell you something, there was a sort of fight at the dance hall place and. . . .'

'I know, I know.'

'I bet you don't. The girl in the shop where I got the polish, she was at the dance and she said that there were these two groups and they started getting cross with each other. . . .'

'You mean mobs, gangs?'

'No I *don't*. I mean groups, silly. Groups that play music. With musical instruments,' Sue added just in case her brother still hadn't grasped the point. 'Well, the first group usually plays at the dances but the second group said they'd been promised a chance to play as well, only they weren't.'

'Weren't what?' Barny asked, painstakingly trying to follow Sue's meaning.

'Asked to play. So then they began shouting and it all got very nasty so this girl left, because she says

her mother doesn't like her being mixed up in anything like that. And that's not all. Just stop a tick.'

Sue swerved to a halt, her cheeks red as apples
for they'd been cycling into the wind. Barny
stopped reluctantly a couple of yards further on and
said over his shoulder, 'We haven't got all day you
know, there's a lot to be done.'

Sue pushed her bike up close to her brother's
and nodded towards the roof of Marsh End Station
which they had nearly reached. She said in a low,
somewhat breathless voice, 'Yes, but this is the
important bit. The leader of the second group is
called Red Fletcher and he's Andy's cousin.
There!'

'Well that's not Andy's fault, is it? You can't help
people being your cousin. It wasn't Andy that was
fighting. Now come on for goodness sake, we're
working on the signal-box today . . . and there's
Andy now. P'raps,' Barny looked hard at Sue,
'P'raps it'd be better if we didn't talk about the
fighting and that. OK?'

'But I wanted to know . . . oh, OK then.'

They met the Senior Director of the line just
short of the station. He was carrying a large sack
over his shoulder and Ellie, as usual, was pecking
round his gumboots.

'I've got more oil and a tin of grease, well *nearly* a whole tin, and some more nails, my Dad's big hammer and saw and some seasoned wood. Real good strong wood,' he announced. 'We may need it if the steps up to the box have gone rotten, eh?'

'Do you think the signals'll still work?' Barny asked.

'Don't see why not. Mind, we may have to . . . oh! Oh hallo, Uncle Fletcher, I didn't know you were coming round.'

'No,' Great Uncle Fletcher rose somewhat stiffly from his seat and leant on his stick. 'No my lad, you didn't, eh? You thought you were safe here to go about your ways. You thought as how nobody'd ever find out about what you've been up to on the sly.'

'I was going to tell you, wasn't I? Once every-thing was all done and polished and mended up. I thought you'd be pleased . . . and these are my friends Barny and Sue who've been helping. . . .'

'I don't want to know your friends from London.'

'*Birmingham,*' corrected Barny. 'Sue and me used to live in. . . .'

'I don't care where it was,' Great Uncle Fletcher roared so loudly that Ellie went flapping off to the far end of the platform. 'I blame you just the same for what you done.'

'But, but we've made everything much nicer and better than it was,' said Sue from behind Barny where she had taken refuge from the rage of this strange old man with the red face.

'Ah. I'm not saying there hasn't been good things done. I'm not saying *that*! No, it's the slyness that

I don't care for. The way you've turned part of my station into this. . . .'

And Great Uncle Fletcher, with surprising agility, turned round and with the aid of his stick opened the door of the Booking Office so forcefully it nearly banged-to again.

'That,' he said. 'How you going to talk *that* away, eh?'

The three Directors, keeping well clear of Great Uncle Fletcher's stick, sidled into the small room. When they had left the previous evening it had been spick and span with its floor swept clean and its walls brushed clear of cobwebs and dust. Now it was very different.

The high stool was lying on its side, while the shelf under the ticket window was littered with sweet papers, torn crisp bags, some half-eaten sausage rolls, three overturned plastic cups from which a dark brown sugary liquid had dripped into an open drawer, and several crumpled paper tissues.

Three pairs of horrified and astonished eyes registered all this as Great Uncle Fletcher said awfully, 'And what about over there, eh?'

By the fireplace there were a number of empty cider bottles and empty, flattened tins which had

71

once held soft drinks while on the wall itself was an ugly black scorch mark.

'Well,' said Great Uncle Fletcher, prodding each of the Directors in turn with his stick. 'Well, what you got to say for yourselves. Desecrating railway property in this manner? What you been up to, eh? I'll deal with you first, because this was *my* station and *my* booking office, but after that it'll be your mothers and fathers who'll have their say, and after them,' Great Uncle Fletcher chewed rapidly, 'after that it'll be the Po-lice. Come on, come on I'm waiting!'

The three Directors looked at each other and then at the furious old man and not one of them was able to say a word, because they just couldn't believe that what was happening was true.

'Tck-tck-tck,' said Ellie from the doorway, 'tck-tck-*TCK.*'

5 · Great Uncle Fletcher

Great Uncle Fletcher was a stubborn old man and once he got an idea into his head it took a great deal of argument to get it out again as Andy, Sue and Barny soon discovered.

'Drinking cider,' he said, shaking his head, 'and at your age! I was nearly grown-up before *my* father'd let me have even a sip of it. But children these days *they*'re allowed to do what ever they fancy. Not made to clear up after themselves neither and when I think. . . .'

'We did, we did,' said Sue, suddenly finding her voice. 'We cleared up like anything. We swept and we weeded out the grass and things and we scrubbed and mended and painted, and Barny's got two fingers that have gone quite blue because he banged them with a hammer when he was putting in new bits to the fence, and I've made all proper curtains for the carriage *and* cleaned out all the

73

nasty dirt and dust, and Andy's got the points oiled and. . . .'

Sue drew in a new breath while the other three stared at her, all of them looking remarkably alike in spite of the differences in their ages as they all had their mouths slightly open, 'and we've done more for your old station that you ever did, so there!'

'That's not true,' shouted Great Uncle Fletcher, thumping his stick on the floor, 'she was the best station this side of the Junction, so she was. Best flower-beds, best waiting room, best booking office and cleanest platform. There, eh?'

'Was,' replied Sue, practically jumping up and down. She didn't often lose her temper, but when she did it was quite a frightening business, 'was, was, *was*! We've worked ever so hard and last night the Booking Office was lovely and now it's all nasty and dirty and I hate it. And I hate you too. I hate *all* of you.'

The door was banged so violently it opened again and the stunned listeners heard the light pitter-patter of Sue's retreating footsteps and then another bang which was followed by silence.

'There,' said Barny after a long uneasy pause, 'you've done it now.'

74

'She's upset,' agreed Andy.

'Ah,' said Great Uncle Fletcher. 'Women.'

He poked gingerly at a cider bottle which fell over and rolled across the floor clankety clank until it came to rest against his feet.

'Ah,' he said again. 'Well, eh?'

'It wasn't us, as did this,' said Andy after another long silence, 'She's right. We did get it all cleared up and cleaned. When it was all done and finished I was going to ask you to come over and look. I thought you'd be pleased. It *is* your station.'

'Was, lad, was. If it wasn't you, who was it then?'

'Dunno.'

'It was somebody else, then,' said Great Uncle Fletcher. He stood very upright and cleared his throat, 'Seems as how I might have made a mistake. *Might* have. Go and ask the girl to come back.'

Barny got up and went out and returned a minute later.

'She won't come out,' he said, 'she's in the Ladies Waiting Room and she's shut the door. I think she's crying.'

'Oh dear, oh lor,' said Great Uncle Fletcher. 'Wait here, eh?'

Neither of the other two knew exactly what he said through the keyhole of the Ladies Waiting

Room, but soon afterwards a somewhat red-eyed and extremely dignified Sue rejoined her fellow Directors, sat down primly on the crate and folded her hands in her lap.

'Ah,' said Great Uncle Fletcher, 'I'll join you there, if it's all the same to you, girl.'

'Not at all,' replied Sue with alarming politeness and she shuffled up a bit. The crate creaked a bit with the weight of the pair of them. Andy hoisted himself on to the stool while Barny settled on the coal-scuttle.

'Now then,' said Great Uncle Fletcher, 'if it wasn't the three of you as made this mess, who was it?'

'Somebody else?' suggested Barny.

'A course it was somebody else, I already said that, didn't I? Boy's a fool.'

'No he's not,' Sue contradicted. 'He's very clever.'

'Don't interrupt, girl. You've had your say and just you remember what I told you back there, eh? Well, Andy?'

'Tramps?' Andy suggested doubtfully.

'First time I ever heard of tramps eating sweeties and lemonade out of tins. Nor'd they leave food behind. Well?'

'Locals,' said Andy slowly and began to swing his feet backwards and forwards, as though he was shy about something.

'Ah, now then, maybe we're getting closer to it,' agreed Great Uncle Fletcher, 'not as local as all *that*, but local sort of. Like lads with a van that's painted up like I don't know what and no proper job of work to do.'

'That's not his—anybody's—their fault,' said Andy, kicking harder than ever.

'Nobody said as how it was. All the same they've got the money to buy petrol and banjos and the like, eh?'

'Maybe,' agreed Andy, 'but we don't know. We're only sort of guessing.'

'So we are, so we are,' agreed Great Uncle Fletcher, while Barny and Sue who were all at sea during this conversation looked at each other and decided to keep quiet. They were both rather shaken by the way in which 'their' station had been treated, because it was an unpleasant feeling to know that somebody else had been here and had made such a mess of all their hard work.

'What can we do about it?' Barny asked helplessly, 'I mean we can't *tell* anybody, because well, really, we're not supposed to be here either.'

A gloomy silence fell over the Board of Directors while Great Uncle Fletcher chewed rapidly, his chin resting on the top of his stick. They watched him anxiously, aware that in some mysterious manner he had stopped being a grown-up enemy and had turned into a friend.

Great Uncle Fletcher felt this too and although he would never ever have said so, he was secretly pleased. It was a long time since anybody had depended on him for information and advice, so he chomped harder than ever and then said suddenly, 'Ah. Yes. Well there's no reason as I know of, why *I* shouldn't come round the station a bit to keep my eye on things. Yes, there's the answer then. Me and Gladys'll come round of an evening.'

'Gladys?' whispered Sue to Andy.

'She's a goose.'

'A goose!' exclaimed Barny before he could stop himself.

"Course she's a goose,' Great Uncle Fletcher said irritably, 'Geese are the best watch dogs there are, don't you know anything?'

'But a goose isn't a d. . . .' Barny began and then stopped suddenly as Andy glared at him. Barny sat back on the coal-scuttle shaking his head. One way and another he was learning a great deal about things like tramps and their habits, but that a goose could be as good as a dog really did take a bit of swallowing. He wondered for a moment if this strange old man knew what he was talking about.

' 'Course a goose isn't a dog,' Great Uncle Fletcher said. 'Everybody knows that, 'cept perhaps in this Birmingham of yours. Geese are *birds*, boy. But if you've a tame goose like Gladys, like I has, she won't let nobody near you if they mean any harm. And if you *do* mean harm, she'll know and she'll go for you with her beak and wings and raise a row while she's doing it.

'The Chinese folk,' he added, '*they* know that, they been using geese to look after their treasures for hundreds of years. Yes, me and Gladys, we'll see there's no more of this vandalism nonsense, don't you fret. Now then, how about you showing me the rest of what you've done here, eh?'

Great Uncle Fletcher certainly made a very good audience as the Directors took him round their work. He prodded at the newly freed points and said they certainly seemed to move quite well. But he shook his head over the frame and showed with his stick where they had badly scored the wheels from applying the brakes too hard.

'It jolly well was *too* hard,' agreed Andy, rubbing his shoulders which were still sore.

'Gently lad, gently,' said Great Uncle Fletcher. 'You can't expect a great mass of metal to come to a halt too quick. It's travelling with all its weight behind it. Even a chap as is running in a race can't stop dead when he comes to the end of it. I heard a fellow on the wireless say as how these big new oil tankers'll take up to more than a mile afore they can stop 'em. It's the same with a frame in its own way. You've got to allow for it, eh?'

'Yes,' agreed Barny, frowning very hard, 'I've seen the machines in the factory where my Dad works. You can't put them into reverse too quickly or they seize up. I hadn't thought of that.'

'Maybe you're not such a fool as I said,' Great Uncle Fletcher grunted, a remark which surprisingly made Barny go quite red with pleasure.

'Well you've seen the station roof and the fence and the points,' put in Sue, 'so now it's my turn. Go on, look at my—our—railway carriage.'

'Coach,' corrected Great Uncle Fletcher and climbed with surprising agility into the Directors' conference chamber. He walked round it slowly, shaking his head and sighing softly while Sue almost trod on his heels, an anxious line across her forehead.

'Well then,' said Great Uncle Fletcher, seating himself in the dining-car, 'I'll tell you this, girl. In my day this was a third class compartment—they don't have 'em now—but to me it looks just like the *first* class. You've not done badly. Not badly at all. Well that's enough of that. What are your next plans, eh?'

There was a hurried whispered conference down the far end of the carriage during which Great Uncle Fletcher gazed out of the window across the weedy tracks towards the main buildings of Marsh End which had once been his pride and joy.

In his mind's eye he saw the busy, puffing steam trains come bustling up the platform and the passengers getting in and out with their piles of luggage. He saw his two porters pushing their trolleys backwards and forwards while his ticket collector stood by the gate and he himself had a word with the driver and the guard. But now it was all empty and quiet, unless that dratted hen could be counted as something, and it wasn't at all the same. . . .

'Here,' said the voice of Andy, 'Great Uncle Fletcher, we've voted and we've decided three to nil, seeing as how Marsh End was your station and that, that we'd like you to join us on the Board. If you'd like to.'

'What's that mean, eh? I'm not joining anything that I don't understand,' said Great Uncle Fletcher gruffly. 'Sit down and tell me just exactly what you mean, boy.'

It took quite a lot of explaining and a lunch meant for three had to be shared between four (although luckily both Mrs Roberts and Mrs Fletcher had been very generous as to the amount of sandwiches that they had provided), before an understanding was reached.

'Ah,' said Great Uncle Fletcher, 'I see then. You're wanting me to be a technical adviser. Well I dunno, I dunno, I'm sure.'

'And security guard,' put in Barny. 'You and — and Gladys.'

'Ah,' Great Uncle Fletcher rubbed his chin, ''Tisn't legal you realize. We've none of us the *right* to be here, but. . . .'

'You mean you won't help after all?' Barny interrupted. He managed to get his fingers out of the way the merest split second before Great Uncle Fletcher's stick thumped the table top.

'But,' said the Newest Director, 'seeing as how

you mean only good things for the Line and also seeing as how you're not *trained* railwaymen and therefore in need of a bit of advice—and added to which,' and Great Uncle Fletcher's thick eyebrows drew together like a pair of furry white caterpillars, 'seeing as how I won't have any banjo-playing do-no-goods making a mess of *my* Marsh End, I accept. Now then, what's your plans, eh?'

'The signal-box.'

'Freeing the next set of points.'

'Clearing up the Booking Office.'

'There's a great deal to be done then, eh?' said Great Uncle Fletcher. 'So we'd best make out a list. Who's a good hand at writing?' He gave an unexpected cackle of laughter and rubbed his chin with the back of his hand.

'What's the matter?' asked Barny, flipping open his notebook and licking his pencil.

'Me,' said Great Uncle Fletcher. 'Imagine me at my time of life being made a Director of the Line! Well, let's get on with it, boy. . . .'

It was surprising how much difference it made having a professional railwayman on the Board as, naturally enough, he knew exactly how things should be done. However he also managed to hold back some of his opinions and Barny, who had been

84

a little afraid that the ex-station master might take over the whole business of re-organizing the Secret Railway, soon stopped worrying on this point.

'You'll have to inspect the signal-box,' said Great Uncle Fletcher, holding the notes at arm's length. 'Get up those steps at my time of life I can't, and you'd best mind as some of 'em'll be rotten, I shouldn't wonder. It'd be a treat to see those signals working again and the level crossing gates too.'

'What about the road?' Barny asked, 'wouldn't it be dangerous if the gates were closed across it?'

"Tisn't a road any more, no more than this is a working station. It went out of use at the same time and it's barricaded off at both ends, and Madam Nature she's done her bit too. You get good blackberries growing there in the Autumn, don't you, Andy?'

'Um,' said Andy, who had remained strangely silent, for him, during the last half hour. Uncle Fletcher had noticed this, but Barny was too wrapped up in his own thoughts while Sue was busy with her plans and she now burst out, 'But what about my—our—Booking Office? I worked ever so hard to get it straight and. . . .'

'Yes, yes, yes, yes,' agreed Great Uncle Fletcher,

'I'll come along with you, girl, and we'll see what the pair of us can do, eh?'

They managed to do a great deal between the two of them and when Great Uncle Fletcher pointed out that he'd be able to collect some money on the empty cider bottles which could go into the fund, Sue's spirits became quite recovered. Especially when she found that Ellie had obligingly laid an egg among the litter of sweet wrappings.

Andy and Barny worked equally hard repairing the steps and the town boy's opinion of the country boy rose as he saw how deftly Andy worked. But the biggest moment of triumph was when they reached the box and had a bird's eye view of the surrounding countryside.

'We can see for miles,' Barny exclaimed. 'Isn't it flat, though?'

'Not as flat as all that. There's the old Marsh, see?'

Andy pointed and Barny following the direction of his finger, nodded. It spread away from them towards the east coast and ultimately the sea, looking for all the world like a green draughtboard with its criss-crossing of ditches and hedges, while behind them the land rose slightly and was more undulating and of a different shade of green, even in the fading winter light.

'*Of course*,' Barny said slowly, 'I never thought of that before. That's why this station is called Marsh *End* . . . and why there's the slope. . . .'

'Gradient!'

'Yes, gradient down to Aldport.'

'They say it was all sea once upon a time and that Dutchmen came over from Holland to show how to drain off the water, but that was a long time ago, hundreds of years I daresay. Well, let's have a look at these signals then. Oh dear,' Andy shook his head, sounding just like his Great Uncle. 'Oh dear, oh me. They're rusted all right, eh? It'll take time to get 'em working properly.'

'We could try,' replied Barny and gripped hold of one of the levers and pulled with all his strength. He grew very red in the face and there was a protesting screeching sound, but that was all.

'Leave off,' said Andy, 'it won't do any good trying to force it. There's a lot to be done before we get 'em working right.'

'OK,' Barny wiped his arm across his forehead and grinned at his friend in the gathering twilight, 'well it doesn't matter, eh? We've got plenty of time to put things straight.'

6 · The phantom train

What with one thing and another it was quite late by the time that Barny and Sue arrived home that evening. They were very tired, but so full of all they'd done that they were still talking when they walked into the front room of their home. Their father had got rolls of paper spread across the table and was frowning over them with a tall thin man whom Barny recognized slightly.

'Oh there you are,' said Mr Roberts, straightening up. 'Do you know what time it is?'

'About seven, but Dad. . . .'

'Do you know your mother's been getting very anxious about you?'

'No, but Dad. . . .'

'Where have you been?'

'Er,' Barny swallowed, 'out. But Dad. . . .

'Out where?'

'Exploring.'

88

'Exploring *what*?'

'Just exploring,' said Barny and Sue added:

'Marsh End. It's a—a place.'

'Marsh End!' exclaimed the tall thin visitor, entering the conversation for the first time. 'Dear me, Marsh End. Now that rings a distant bell in my mind. Marsh End . . . let me think. Yes, *got* it. There was a through station there, twin track and run by the old Great Eastern. Let me see, the trains called at Durnham, Durnham West, Draxmundham, Lower Draxmundham, the Junction—naturally— and then Higher Marsh, Marsh End, West Aldport, Aldport Central. Right?'

There was a stunned silence and the visitor fiddled with his spectacles and murmured, 'I'm so sorry, but it was always one of my favourite lines. I learnt it as a boy, when Bradshaw's Railway Guide was the apple of my eye. I was very sad when they stopped printing Bradshaw. It was so interesting to work out theoretical journeys. Well. And there we are. How do you do?'

'This,' said Mr Roberts, recovering his bearings with some difficulty, 'is Mr Denton from Head Office. He's staying at the Aldport Arms.'

Everybody shook hands and while Mr Roberts rolled up the blueprints Mr Denton put his fingers together to form a church spire and looked over his spectacles at Barny and Sue. For once in their lives they could think of nothing at all to say.

'You must forgive me,' said Mr Denton, 'railways were once a hobby of mine. Indeed they still are in a manner of speaking as I belong to various Groups, but it's not the same since the end of steam. However, Mr Roberts, as your family have now returned safely I mustn't take up any more of your time. In any case I have to make out a full report. It's a pity, a great pity, but obviously the entire scheme is going to be uneconomic. Good night. Marsh End, dear me.'

Barny and Sue continued to look silently at each other until their father returned. Then Barny said hesitantly, 'I'm awfully sorry we were so late Dad, we didn't see how late it was. Who was—I mean what did Mr Denton mean?'

'Mr Denton,' said Barny's mother from the kitchen where she was dishing up the supper, 'is an Area Manager and Co-ordinator from GER Plastics and a very clever man indeed. Go and wash your hands the pair of you—wherever you've been exploring is a nasty dirty place—and after that your Dad's got some news that you'll like. Hurry up do or your meal'll be spoilt.'

'What news, Dad?' Barny asked as they sat down round the table.

'Well, boy,' Mr Roberts said slowly, 'it's like this. I've drawn up my plans as to what GER could do round here—the off-shore rig as I told you—and I've had a look at where we could build a factory. And all that's OK. But it still seems that we can't get enough workers into the area.'

'Why?'

'Well, there's enough of them, but transportation, as I told you, is the difficulty. We can't depend on what the firm calls a regular work force or a good road system, so the whole scheme's down the drain. It's no skin off our nose and, from your way of looking at things, I daresay, it's all to the good because it means we'll be moving back to Birmingham. Which is what the two of you want, isn't it?'

Barny opened his mouth to reply and then stopped because suddenly it occurred to him that it wasn't all right at all. He didn't really want to leave Aldport, which wasn't too bad a sort of place once you got used to it. In particular he would hate to leave the Secret Railway just when they'd started to get it looking and working right. Anyway, how would Andy and Great Uncle Fletcher manage—

even with the help of Gladys—if Marsh End were to be invaded again and more damage done?

Added to which he'd really been looking forward to getting the signal-box into prime condition and pulling the levers so that the far signals would work and the gates would grind into action. There was also the tricky business of finding a better way to halt the frame and they hadn't even touched on that old engine in its shed and. . . .

'No!' the word erupted out of Sue. 'No, no, NO. I don't want to go back to Birmingham. I've just got the Booking Office nice again and OH!'

'Whatever's the matter with you?' asked Mrs Roberts in astonishment.

'I want to stay here,' wailed Sue, 'because I'm going to mend the cushions, oh, oh, OH!'

'Thoroughly overtired,' said Mrs Roberts, 'I *knew* we shouldn't've let them go gallivanting off round the countryside like this. Now blow your nose and stop being a silly cry-baby.

Although,' and Mrs Roberts quite spoilt the effect of her words by adding, 'although I understand in a way, because I'll be sorry to leave Aldport myself. That nice woman down at the supermarket —the one who's got the daughter that went to that dance as I told you, Ted—well she's asked me if I'd like to join the Women's Institute and to show them how to make Edgbaston buns. . . .'

'It's not a bad sort of place, I'll grant you that,' agreed Mr Roberts. 'Quiet, agreed, but old Harry Fletcher, you wouldn't know him, well he's promised to take me fishing for sea trout in the Stour and perhaps a bit of pike, roach and rudd in the Blyth. Then there's the off-shore fishing too. Did you know that with the North Atlantic drift round this part of East Anglia you can get good crabs and lobsters with—the—right—pots. . . .'

Mr Roberts' voice drifted into silence as he realized that the other three members of his family were watching him in astonishment.

'I used to like fishing a bit in the canals round Birmingham when I was a lad,' he went on with a faint sigh, 'but what with the waste from the factories and that there's not much life there any more. Still, that's all in the past, and *we've* got to think about the future. It'll be grand to get back to Birmingham and all our old friends, won't it?'

'Yes,' said Mrs Roberts, 'oh yes it will. Get on with your supper now.'

'Yes,' said Sue, her mouth turned down at the corners.

But Barny didn't say anything at all, added to

93

which his appetite had quite gone away, which was most unusual for him. He had a great deal on his mind and the end result was that at ten o'clock the following morning Great Uncle Fletcher, stumping across the fields from his cottage, was intercepted by Barny.

'I say,' said Barny, 'we're going.'

'Are you indeed. And where to, may I ask? You nearly run over my feet then, boy.'

'Sorry,' Barny slid off his bike. 'I say, was everything OK last night?'

"Twas. Gladys and me came round on our patrol latish and it was all as quiet as a March Hare in February. Go on, boy.'

'There's not the right sort of work force, that is people to do the work, round about Marsh End, so the firm my father works for isn't going to build a factory and because of that he won't be working here, well that is Aldport, any more, so we'll be leaving.'

'And you don't want to, eh?'

'Well I did, once upon a time, but not any more.'

'Why?'

'I dunno,' Barny kicked at a stone, his head bent over the handlebars of his bike. 'It's sort of all right here and I like the station and working on it, eh?'

'Eh,' agreed Great Uncle Fletcher, 'there goes another skein of geese. It's tidy the way they fly. Orderly. The summer birds'll be back soon I shouldn't wonder. Spring's coming. So what do you mean to do about it, boy?'

'There's nothing I *can* do,' Barny said with an enormous sigh. 'If we've got to go back to Birmingham, that's that.'

'Tell me about it,' said Great Uncle Fletcher, 'and don't go thinking it's the end of the world because t'aint. There's a lot worse fish in the sea than you'll ever know of. . . .'

It did Barny a great deal of good to talk, and he did a lot of it as they made their way to Marsh End. Great Uncle Fletcher hardly spoke at all, apart from a grunt here and there, and at the finish he only said, 'Well there 'tis then. We've all got our troubles, eh? And if you want to get those signals working you'd best take some grease up to the box. Where's your sister, eh?'

Sue, equally doleful, arrived an hour later together with Andy who appeared to have the cares of the world on his shoulders.

'If ever I see such a threesome,' said Great Uncle Fletcher, thumping his stick so violently that Ellie ran squawking from cover into the Ladies Waiting

Room. 'You've not the one of you got the backbone of a slow-worm and so I'm telling you. Get on with it do, eh? We won't never have this station working properly if you don't get down to it.

'Oh dear, oh lor, oh me,' he sighed, 'how am I going to get those signals going or those points moving nice and easy, let alone the gates? You're as lazy and as good-for-nothing a bunch as I've ever seen. Bless me if I couldn't do it all myself and a sight better, but then you children today haven't got any get up and go, let alone self-discipline. You want everything done for you. . . .'

But long before Great Uncle Fletcher had finished speaking his fellow directors, rigid with fury and a desire to show him that he was speaking nonsense, had disappeared in all directions and within a very few minutes Marsh End was a hive of industry. Platforms were being swept, points oiled and greased and weeds cleared at a quite astonishing rate, while Ellie, her wings half spread, was running from place to place adding to the din.

It wasn't until dusk was falling over the landscape that Andy shouted from the signal-box, 'Oi, hang about, *BARNY*!'

'Um?'

'I think she'll work. Come up, eh?'

Barny dropped his spade, hesitated for a second and then, picking it up and putting it over his shoulder, doubled off towards the signal-box, as Uncle Fletcher shouted:

'Right, I'm with you. There's the through train from Draxmundham on the down line. Are you ready, eh?'

It was a thrilling moment, even allowing for the fact that any engine on the down line must be a phantom one. Barny, his eyes shining with excitement, glanced at Andy who nodded silently, and Barny pulled down the handles. There was a satisfying click-click as the B signals went into action.

'Your level crossing, boy.' roared the voice of Great Uncle Fletcher.

'Oh dear, oh lor,' mumbled Andy and turned the wheel.

There was a protesting scream and by the brightening light of the rising moon the personnel of Marsh End saw the grey-white gates groan protestingly into action. It was a long, long time since they had been made to move and although they had been cleared of weeds and oiled into the bargain they moved with a kind of shuddering moan.

'Signal B,' hissed Barny.

'Signal B,' replied Andy.

'Signal D on the down line.'

'Signal D.'

Click, clack, thump.

Amazingly the old signals, rusted and uncared for, squeaked and thudded into action like old war-horses which had heard the bugle blowing for business.

'Oh my, oh dear, oh lor,' said Great Uncle Fletcher. 'She's coming through, listen girl. . . .'

Sue grasped her dustpan and brush and held her breath. It was very, very quiet out on the Marsh, so quiet that she almost fancied that she could hear the distant sea breaking on the stony beaches of Aldport.

'Listen do, eh?' said Great Uncle Fletcher.

Was there or was there not far out towards

Draxmundham a faint shrill whistle? And weren't the rails starting to twang softly as if a steam engine was pounding towards them?

'It's very real, isn't it?' Sue whispered.

'It's more'n that,' Great Uncle Fletcher replied. 'There's someone coming.'

Up in the signal box Barny strained his eyes, as he peered towards the setting sun.

'Hey, Andy,' he said hoarsely. 'I can hear something. . . .'

'It's imagination, eh?'

'No, 'tisn't,' Barny put his hand behind his ear, 'Something's coming—and fast too, but not on the railway line. On the *ROAD*. Andy, put up the gates —QUICK!'

7 · Red for danger

For what seemed a very long time to the four horrified watchers Andy heaved with all his might at the wheel. But the gates didn't appear to move. Sue, who had climbed up to the signal-box, put her hands over her ears and shut her eyes tightly, but Barny stared down at the darkening landscape, unable to look away.

A car was moving fast down the old road, and the driver obviously knew it well for he had no head-lights on. He looked like a black shadow as Barny caught glimpses of him through the high leafless hedges.

'I can't bear it, I can't bear it,' Sue whispered. 'He's going to crash and it'll be our fault. . . .'

'Shut up,' Barny said fiercely, which was pointless really as of course she couldn't hear him. And then the gates were swinging back and came to rest parallel with the hedges. At the same moment the car came fully into sight for the first time and Andy exclaimed, 'It's my cousin Red! It's his van.'

The van thudded to a standstill some yards further on and then the engine was switched off and a door banged violently.

'What was that?' asked Sue, jumping clean off the floor with fright.

'Everything's OK,' Barny bellowed in her face and nodded violently as she reluctantly opened her eyes and took her hands away from her ears.

'I'll go down,' Andy said hoarsely, 'put everything straight, Barny. I'd better see him.'

Red Fletcher came striding across the station yard and into the main hall just as Andy clambered up on to the platform.

'You young idiot,' shouted his cousin, 'you nearly killed me, mucking about with those gates. Just wait till I get my hands on you. . . .'

He was a well built young man in his late teens and now with his face bunched up with rage and his hands clenched into fists, he was enough to scare anyone, let alone a much younger and slighter boy. Andy swallowed, but stood his ground as Red raised one large hand as though to cuff him across the head.

'Just you stop that, lad,' said the quiet voice of

Great Uncle Fletcher from the shadows. Red swung round, as light as a cat on his feet and then laughed as he said, 'Oh it's you, is it? I might have known.'

'And that'll be enough of your impudence,' Great Uncle Fletcher replied. 'And anyway what were *you* doing driving down that old lane? You know as well as I do that it's closed to traffic.'

'That's my business!'

'Ah, is it then? Well so is it our business if we want to use the level crossing gates. There!'

Red Fletcher hesitated and then turned back to the silent Andy.

'I see how it is,' he said in a jeering voice. 'You're playing at railways again, aren't you? I'd have thought you were a bit old to be doing kids' games.'

'It's not a game,' Andy said miserably. 'It's, it's. . . .'

'Who's there?' Red pushed his cousin aside and peered across the track as Barny and Sue picked their way over it. 'Oh, more kids! Is that the lot of you, then?'

'Yes,' Barny said huskily. He didn't like the look of Red Fletcher at all. He reminded Barny all too clearly of the gangs of older teenagers who used to start teasing and jeering at his own group of friends in Birmingham. There had been some very nasty moments, but because he'd had so many friends to back him up there'd never been any real trouble.

But this was different. There was only him and Andy to deal with things as Sue and Great Uncle Fletcher could hardly be counted as being very adequate support.

Unfortunately Sue, who was still suffering slightly from shock at the near accident, now said the first thing which came into her mind which was: 'You're Red Fletcher, aren't you? The one who did the fighting at the dance and broke all the windows. Oh dear!'

'That's right,' Red stuck his thumbs into his belt and tilted backwards on his heels. 'So you've heard about me, have you?'

'It's nothing to be proud of,' snapped Great Uncle Fletcher. 'Vandalism, that's what it is. It was you and your precious friends as was here a couple of nights ago, I daresay.'

'Right again,' agreed Red, sounding proud of the fact. 'And what's more we'll be coming back. It's not a bad little place this for practising our numbers. Anyway there's nowhere else, seeing as how they won't let us play down at the dance hall. They promised they'd give us an audition and then they went back on their word. 'Tisn't fair, eh?'

'And it isn't fair of you,' said Barny, suddenly finding his tongue, 'to come and muck up all our work.'

'Isn't it, ooooh!' said Red. 'What right have you got to be here then, playing at trains?'

'As much right as you,' said Barny, shaking off Sue's trembling hand which was grabbing at his arm.

'Prove it,' Red pushed his head forward and Barny retreated and very nearly fell off the edge of the platform. 'Prove it, eh? You're trespassers just the same as us but I've got my group behind me, see? There's four of us same as there are of you. That's fair, eh? So do you want to make a fight of it or don't you?'

There was a long silence while everybody weighed up the odds and then Andy said in a tired voice, 'OK Red, you win. You can take over Marsh End. I don't care.'

'Andy!' Barny exclaimed.

Andy shuffled his feet and looked over his friend's head as he said heavily, 'He's my cousin isn't he, eh?'

Andy turned away, his gumboots shuffling along the platform.

'No,' Barny shouted, 'no, you can't mean that. Andy. . . .'

'Oh yes he does.'

A heavy hand gripped hold of Barny and swung him round so that he was looking up into Red's face.

'You're new to these parts, aren't you? A foreigner, eh? Well, I was born here and I reckon that gives me more right to be here than you. Besides, you're only messing about playing trains. Me and my group, we need the station to work in. It's only right I should have Marsh End—I'm a lot more important than you kids.'

'Even if you haven't got regular work,' said the tart voice of Great Uncle Fletcher from the shadows.

'Ah, shut up,' Red said furiously. ''Tisn't 'cos I haven't tried. Only there *isn't* any work round here. I should know, I tried everywhere in Aldport. If I didn't have the group, I'd go barmy with nothing to do. Anyway,' and he let go of Barny so suddenly that Barny sagged to his knees, 'I like running a group and one day we'll be successful and on the telly, you'll see.'

Sue, who had only followed about half of all that

was said, went running off after Andy and caught up with him just as he reached the station yard. The van, its violent colours reduced to shades of grey by the moonlight, was parked by the entrance.

'Andy,' Sue said breathlessly, '*don't* let him do it. Don't let him take Marsh End away . . .' her voice rose on the last few words. 'Oh Andy, please don't.'

'Let me go,' Andy said, shaking away her hand, 'I can't stop him, *we* can't stop him. Don't you see that? He'll just bring all his friends over and they'll wreck the lot—all we've done and more. Do you want it to be like that? Do you, eh? Do you want to see Marsh End made into a proper right old shambles? He'd do it too, you know he would, don't you?'

Sue's jaw went up and down, just in the same way that Great Uncle Fletcher's did when he was worked up about something. She hardly took any notice when Ellie came fluttering and complaining across the yard to join them.

'I don't, I don't,' said Sue, 'oh dear, oh me. . . .'

Andy stumped off into the silvery darkness, Sue watched him vanish and then she pulled her wrist across her face and said in a furious although somewhat wobbly whisper, 'I don't care. I don't care at all. They're not going to make a horrid nasty mess of the station and *my* curtains and *my* cushions and, and, and everything. So there!'

'Vandalism,' said Great Uncle Fletcher and banged his stick down on the platform. 'I won't have it, not here at Marsh End.'

'There's nothing you can do to stop it,' Red replied, 'nothing. Well, good night all.'

'Nothing?' asked Barny in a low voice as Red's soft footsteps vanished into the darkness to be followed by the sound of the van starting up.

'Not much,' said Great Uncle Fletcher. 'I suspected all along as how it was Red and his friends, and Andy suspected the same, I could tell. I had thought we might scare 'em off, Gladys and me, but even if we did they'd be back. And, you see lad, there'd be family trouble, and Andy'd be in the middle of it all. I'm not saying who's in the right or wrong of it, but it'd be Andy's father having to speak up to Red's father and it all makes for bad feeling. Andy, he sees that. So don't you go thinking too badly about him, eh?'

Barny heaved up a deep sigh and Great Uncle Fletcher very gently put a hand on his shoulder as he said. 'It's the way of the world, lad. But we had a bit of fun while it was going, eh?'

'Eh,' agreed Barny, 'but all the same it's not *fair*.'

'I shan't,' said Barny furiously about thirty minutes later as he and Sue pedalled into Aldport. 'I shan't like it at all and I don't want to go back and I don't think Dad does either, nor Mum, nor you. Do you?'

But Sue didn't reply. She only leant further over her handlebars, her mouth turned right down at the corners and with two brilliant splashes of colour in her cheeks. She didn't in the least understand all the ins and outs of what had occurred and neither did she care. The only thing that was on her mind was that nobody and nothing mattered except all the time and trouble that she had taken over the refurnishing of Marsh End—and, she was stonily determined, nothing was going to undo her work! Nothing, nothing, NOTHING!

During the next two days Mr and Mrs Roberts realized that their children were not at all happy. Barny was in a far worse temper than he had been since they first came to live at Aldport. He would hardly speak a word to anyone, while his appetite appeared to have vanished completely. It was a unique state of affairs which made Mrs Roberts say to her husband, 'He *must* be sickening for something. We'd better send for the doctor, Ted. I don't like it.'

'Perhaps he doesn't want to leave Aldport after all,' said Mr Roberts, stroking the fishing rod that he'd bought, with a regretful sigh. 'I must admit I'll be sorry to go too in a way.'

'And then there's Sue,' went on Mrs Roberts. 'Now, she's not usually a sulky sort of girl. With her it's normally a right old bit of temper and tantrums and then everything's all right again. But now she's brooding. I tell you I don't like it Ted.'

'She'll be all right,' growled Mr Roberts, as he started to take his rod to pieces. 'Let's get on with the packing, there's a lot to be done.'

8 · Green for go

It took three full days for the Directors of the Secret Railway to shake off their crushing sense of defeat. It always takes time to recover from a shock but, by the evening of that third doleful day, all four of them had reached a secret decision *not* to just sit down and admit that they were beaten, but to jolly well make a fight of it, no matter what the consequences might be. As none of them wanted to get his or her fellow directors into trouble they didn't say a word about their individual plans.

Great Uncle Fletcher was the first to make a move. He opened his front door, sniffed the fresh morning air and muttered under his breath, 'Spring's a-coming. I can smell it. Gladys! Gladys, I say!'

Gladys came running and cackling out of her shed with her great wings half-spread, her head sideways on so that one round eye was fixed on her master's craggy face.

112

'Now listen here, you,' said Great Uncle Fletcher, buttoning his coat right up to the neck, as spring coming or not it was still distinctly nippy at seven o'clock in the morning. 'I'm off, I am.'

'Kaaark,' agreed Gladys, stretching her long neck still further.

'Be quiet and listen, you silly great fowl, or I'll have you for my Christmas dinner, so I will.'

'Kaaark,' said Gladys, who'd heard this threat many times before.

'I daresay. I'm a-going to pay a call on my eldest nephew, stupid great chunkhead that he is, even if he does call himself an agricultural machinery expert. *Expert!*' Great Uncle Fletcher snorted loudly. 'I'd like to see him maintaining a 4–6–OT proper. That's a *real* expert job that is. Still he's young Red's father, so he's the one that'll have to sort this out, first off. They'll have to learn to share Marsh End, turn and turn about. It's the only sensible answer. And while I'm gone, just you keep your eyes on things. Right, eh?'

'Kaaark,' agreed Gladys and fluffed out her feathers as she escorted Great Uncle Fletcher to the garden gate.

'And wish me luck.'

'Kaaark.'

113

H

Exactly twenty-nine minutes after this happened, Andy slipped silently out of his home and, looking remarkably like his Great Uncle in spite of the difference in their ages, he too set off across the fields. His objective was the same and he was a great deal more scared because he knew that his Uncle 'Ginger' Fletcher's fiery temper was treated with respect throughout the district.

'It's for the sake of the Secret Railway, the sake of the Secret Railway,' Andy kept muttering under his breath. He shivered violently as he walked and was so engrossed in what he was doing that he never heard Gladys give him a friendly hiss-hoot as he marched on across the Marsh which was dappled with fading shadows.

Fifteen minutes after *this*, the Second Senior Director of the line climbed on to his bicycle and began to pedal through the still deserted streets of Aldport, with a great many pieces of cardboard and two rolls of paper strapped across his saddle-bag. *His* destination was the Aldport Arms, which was the largest building in the town and really quite an awe-inspiring place. Barny parked his bike carefully between an elderly Rolls and a shining new Cortina and walked into the entrance hall.

114

'Newspapers round the back, sonny,' said the Hall Porter.

'I'm not the newspapers,' said Barny, 'I'm a—a—visitor and I'd like to see Mr Denton. Please.'

'Get on,' said the Hall Porter. 'At this time of the morning?'

'It's urgent. A matter of business, eh?' said Barny.

'Ah,' the Hall Porter scratched his chin and frowned. 'You're not selling anything or up to any mischief?'

'No.'

'Ah. Well.'

There was another long pause during which Barny quite distinctly heard both the rattle of cutlery in the kitchens and the fast banging noise of his own heart.

'What name shall I say?' asked the Hall Porter, very slowly reaching for the telephone.

'Roberts,' said Barny.

'And type of business?'

'Marsh End and GER.'

'All right. I'll *call* Mr Denton. But if this *is* a leg-pull I'll have your guts for garters as the saying goes. Hang on a minute, eh?'

'Eh,' agreed Barny and would have crossed his fingers only they were trembling too much. All kinds of dreadful ideas swam through his mind as he watched the number being dialled. Mr Denton being furious, Barny's father being summoned, even, (and Barny swallowed painfully) his father being demoted and returned to the shop floor at GER.

'Mr Denton, sir,' said the Hall Porter in quite a different voice from the one he had used for Barny, 'I'm sorry to bother you, but there's a young lad here from Marsh End who says he'd like to see you on a matter of what *he* calls business. Name of Roberts. . . .'

And at that exact moment Sue, the youngest Director of the Secret Railway, having looked everywhere for Barny and given him up as a bad job, set off on *her* journey. She was the only one of the four of them who had Marsh End as a target, and her mouth was turned right down at the corners.

Meanwhile, Great Uncle Fletcher and Andy, having had a head start so to speak, were carrying out a united attack on a somewhat bemused Uncle Ginger Fletcher and a very angry Red Fletcher.

'Now hold on, hold on,' said Uncle Ginger Fletcher, raising one enormous hand. 'Let me get this straight, eh? Young Red here and little Andy there. . . .'

'I'm *not* little,' said Andy, trying to get up out of his kitchen chair. The hands of his uncle and his great uncle fell on his shoulders and Andy not only sat down with a thump, but very nearly vanished under the table.

'Shut up do,' said Great Uncle Fletcher, 'or I'll catch you one.'

'So'll I,' agreed Uncle Ginger. 'The two of 'em have been using that old Marsh End Station for their games. Right?'

'*Games!*' said Red, 'It's not *games* with me and my Group. *We're* not playing at railways. We're practising, we're. . . .'

The hands of his father and his great uncle came to rest on him too and Red stopped talking very quickly. He shot a look across the table at his youngest cousin and just for a second they weren't enemies any longer, but allies.

'So?' said Uncle Ginger Fletcher.

'So,' echoed Great Uncle Fletcher calmly, 'it's a big station, why can't they share it, eh?'

There was a long pause while the three generations of Fletchers thought over this idea.

'I dunno,' said Uncle Ginger Fletcher.

117

'I dunno,' agreed his son Red.

'I dunno at all,' said Andy.

'Give me patience, do,' said Great Uncle Fletcher with an enormous sigh. 'We're all *tres*passing, aren't we? None of us has the *right* to be there. What me and my fellow directors were trying to do was to. . . .'

'Your *what*?' asked Uncle Ginger Fletcher.

'Fellow Directors,' continued Great Uncle Fletcher, 'of GER, if you'll kindly let me say my piece, young Ginger. What we was trying to do was to get Marsh End back into respectable shape. WE was aiming to get it into running order. While you, Red, only meant harm and destruction for it.'

'Turn the record over. Me and my Group need that place while you and your lot are only playing games,' said Red very rudely and then ducked as his father's ham-like fist whistled past his ear.

'*Will* you be quiet!' roared Ginger Fletcher.

'Our games are only good for the railway and the rolling-stock,' said Andy, 'while your lot just damage 'em, eh?'

'Who says?' whispered Red.

'I do,' replied Great Uncle Fletcher, whose deafness appeared to have vanished for the moment—as it usually did when it suited him. 'Now just you

118

all be quiet and listen, for I'm tired of your noise. Marsh End was my station once and I was proud of it, which is something you'll none of you ever understand, except perhaps Andy here because he likes railways, same as I do. His friends, they feel the same too, even if they *are* foreigners. We've offered you the hand o'friendship but if you won't take it, then that's that, eh?'

'We need somewhere to practise,' said Red sulkily.

'The lad's got a point,' agreed his father. 'They won't let 'em play down in Aldport. . . .'

'All right then, turn and turn about at Marsh End, eh?'

'I dunno,' said Red still sounding rather sulky. 'I'll have to consult my Group.'

'Consult, my foot,' said Great Uncle Fletcher getting to his feet. 'You make up your mind here and now, lad, 'cause if you don't I'm off. I'm back to Marsh End to clear out all your rubbish and so I'm telling you. And what's more,' Great Uncle Fletcher's jaws chomped up and down furiously, 'I'm not afraid of you nor your group nor your family and that includes you, young Ginger! You were always more gas than go. Expert indeed! I'd like to see you maintenance a 4–6–OT, my lad.'

'Now Uncle Fletcher. . . .'

'Don't you Uncle Fletcher me,' said Great Uncle Fletcher, working himself up into a royal rage. 'We offered you good terms, so we did, but if you don't want to take 'em. . . .'

Red twisted about in his chair and then said in a not too certain voice, 'Ah well, that isn't all of it, see? I've been back to Marsh End and I've put all our instruments in the old Booking Office and a padlock on the door. I reckon that gives *us*—me and my Group—certain rights, eh?'

There was a long silence during which Andy went white while Great Uncle Fletcher's face turned from red to purple.

'Tea,' said Uncle Ginger hastily, 'let's have a cup of tea and talk a bit more. . . .'

At the same moment Barny was saying to a still bewildered Mr Denton, 'Don't you see? All your freight problems would be solved if you used the railway? The line goes straight through, apart from a bit of a curve that is, and. . . .'

'East of Marsh End,' interrupted Mr Denton, 'where the gradient starts. One in a hundred, if my memory serves me correctly. But no, Barny, no. I'm sorry, boy, but your plan is quite out of the question.'

Mr Denton put the last of his overnight things into his suitcase, snapped it shut and got to his feet.

Barny, with the brand of courage which springs from desperation, placed himself between Mr Denton and the door and with shaking hands unrolled one of the papers he had brought with him.

'At least have a look,' he said huskily.

Mr Denton blinked and then replied mildly,

'Well, I suppose I could . . . only . . . well . . . let's lay that down on the table shall we, where we can both study it . . . er . . . properly. Dear me, it's a map of the district, showing Aldport and the proposed off-shore rig and the possible factory site.'

'It's not very good I know,' said Barny, 'but I had to copy Dad's blueprints in an awful rush and without his knowing. He doesn't know, you know, about any of this, so it's none of it his fault. It's me. Mine.'

'Calm down,' said Mr Denton. 'I believe I'm beginning to grasp the situation. This meeting is the concern of you and me only. We will, therefore, both of us treat it as confidential. However Barny, if you want to put forward a business idea you must learn to do it clearly and concisely.'

'Yes sir,' said Barny, and suddenly he felt less shaky and yet rather sick at the same time.

'I tell you what,' said Mr Denton, looking at Barny over the top of his spectacles, 'as one never does one's best thinking on an empty stomach, supposing we have a bit of breakfast while we talk.'

'Yes, but—and I am sort of hungry—but there isn't much time to talk, because you've got to get back to GER Plastics and . . . I say!' Barny's face turned scarlet right up to his hair. 'I say, Mr Denton. GER—it's the same initials. Your firm's and the

Great Eastern Railway's. G.E.R. You wouldn't even have to change the signs at Marsh End, or along the line! Now, look. . . .'

'That's a thought,' agreed Mr Denton, his eyes twinkling as he picked up the telephone. 'Bacon and eggs?'

'Yes please.'

Barny unrolled the second paper and held it out flat with hands which were no longer trembling, 'Now this is my friend Andy Fletcher's drawing of the line. Of course it's not to scale, sir, but it will give you an idea of—of . . .' Barny sought for the right word and then finished triumphantly, 'the layout.'

Mr Denton put down the telephone and joined Barny at the table. He studied both plans, going 'm m m' under his breath while Barny held his and then he took a couple of ornaments off the mantelpiece to anchor the ends of one map more securely and went 'm m m' again and snapped his fingers. Barny looked hopefully round the hotel bedroom, and then as there were no more weighty objects in sight, he slipped off his shoes and used them to hold the second paper in place.

Mr Denton pursed his lips, looked over his

spectacles and then through them and then stared at Barny.

'Here,' said Barny, in a high squeaky voice which he hardly recognized as his own, 'here is Durnham from which there's still a direct line to Birmingham New Street. It's a commuter line which also carries freight.'

'Agreed.'

'So all you, I mean GER Plastics have to do, is to re-open this line from Durnham to Aldport. It goes straight through and it's twin track at Marsh End. And,' Barny warmed to his subject, 'it needn't only *be* freight. There's an awful lot of people who live quite near the railway stations along the line who could reach it easily and come into the factory at Aldport by train. If you build a factory, that is. Well?'

'M m m,' said Mr Denton. 'It's an *idea*. I won't go further than that. Ah—breakfast! Open the door, Barny.'

Barny did as he was told and then as the waiter put down the laden tray on the bed, he added, 'Well?'

'Breakfast,' said Mr Denton, 'let's have a cup of tea and think things over.'

'But there may not be time,' said Barny rather desperately.

'Time? It's all right, I'm not in any particular hurry. You mustn't try and stampede me, Barny. Or,' and Mr Denton's voice sharpened, 'Are you worried about something—or somebody—else?'

Barny shuffled the small pieces of cardboard which he had brought with him and which were marked 'Freight trains' and 'Passenger trains' and decided he had better tell the whole truth. That there was another contender for the use of Marsh End, Red Fletcher.

'Well,' said Barny, gazing fixedly at a large sea-gull which was perched on a chimney-pot, 'well, there *is* one *other* thing I'd better tell you.'

'I thought there might be. Go on.'

'There's another lot of people who want to take over Marsh End,' said Barny, still addressing the seagull. 'In fact they may be there already.'

But he was quite wrong as someone else had got there first, the third director of the Line having already carried out her own private plan.

'That's that then,' said Sue somewhat breath-lessly to Ellie in the shadowy darkness of the

125

Ladies Waiting Room. 'Nobody's going to take away MY Secret Railway from me. Not after all the cleaning up I've done AND the curtains I've made.'

'Tck-tck-tck,' said Ellie encouragingly and fluttered up on to the long seat where Sue was sitting surrounded by various objects.

'I *think* it's what's called a "sit-in",' Sue went on. 'I suppose that's because you're sitting inside somewhere. Anyway, I can stay here for ages and ages because I've brought a lot of food. I just hope Mum

won't get into too much of a state. Oh dear somebody's coming. Oh Ellie!'

Sue bounced up and down nervously and Ellie
went skipping and flying along the seat, scrambled
on to a gleaming guitar, fluffed out her feathers and
slowly settled down firmly.

'I'm a bit scared,' said Sue in a whisper as a car
stopped and doors banged and there was the sound
of footsteps and voices. 'People don't usually do sit-
ins on their own, you see.'

'Tck-tck whhhhhh,' said Ellie.

The voices and the footsteps drew nearer. . . .

9 · All lines clear

'Now then,' said Uncle Ginger. 'You show us, Red, where you've put them musical instruments of yours.'

'Yes, Dad,' said Red with a triumphant glance at Great Uncle Fletcher and Andy, and he clumped towards the Booking Office.

'The lad's right, you know,' said Uncle Ginger. 'If he's got his stuff stacked here then possession *is* nine points of the law. Whatever that may mean,' he added, rather spoiling the weight of his pronouncement.

'The law, as such, doesn't come into it,' said Great Uncle Fletcher, 'seeing as how we're all *outside* it. We're all *tres*passers.'

'So you said, Uncle. All right then, if we're talking about squatters rights, my Red, he's got there first. Eh?'

'I suppose so,' Great Uncle Fletcher agreed grudgingly.

'Bingo,' said Red and undid the large padlock he'd placed on the Booking Office door. He threw the door open and stood aside. Everybody surged into the room and looked about them. Hanging on the hooks were Andy's duffle, some old railway time-tables and a thick wad of papers. Beneath them were a row of lamps and a neatly furled flag. The high stool was still there and the coal hod and scuttle, but apart from that there was nothing to see but an obviously empty crate.

'Well?' said Uncle Ginger Fletcher. 'Where's your guitar and that?'

'*Gone*!' said Red. 'They've *gone*! I've been rob-bed! My group's been robbed! Somebody's stolen all our gear. Who? How?'

'Through that window, I shouldn't be surprised,' said Great Uncle Fletcher, starting to chuckle. 'The Booking Office window is wide open, lad.'

'Nobody could get through there!'

'Oh yes they could,' said Andy. He caught Great Uncle Fletcher's eye and began to smile himself. 'A small sort of person could. Maybe a very small . . .' he stopped short and both he and Great Uncle Fletcher stared at each other and then Andy said in a whisper, 'She couldn't have—she can't have—*can* she?'

129

'She's the littlest,' said Great Uncle Fletcher, chumping up and down, 'and when her temper gets up there's no knowing what she'll get at. Remember the last time, eh?'

'I don't understand,' said Uncle Ginger Fletcher, 'what you're on about. There's none of young Red's stuff here, that's for certain. My word, Uncle Fletcher, you've kept this place neat. I remember when I used to come here as a lad. You'd fine flower-beds then.'

'My gear!' shouted Red. 'All my gear! Where's it gone, eh?'

He sounded so upset that everybody kept quiet for a moment and then all of them turned towards the main door as they heard the sound of an approaching car.

'It's the police,' whispered Red.

'The Railway Police, lad,' corrected Great Uncle Fletcher.

But they were all wrong for a bright and shining Cortina drew up alongside Red's van in the station yard. Out of it stepped a man in a dark suit with a briefcase under his arm and a somewhat pale-faced Barny at his heels.

'Good morning,' said Mr Denton. 'Why you must be Great Uncle, I mean, Mr Fletcher. Good gracious me, I remember you, sir! Why, when I was just a boy I travelled on this line—it was a great many years ago—and you were the Station Master. It must have been some very special occasion, because, as I recall, you were wearing your top hat and tailcoat. Could it have been . . . I beg your pardon.'

'Not at all, sir,' Great Uncle Fletcher replied, leaning on his stick. 'It must have been a Royal visit that you're talking about. When we were steam.'

'A four-six-o?'

' "The Great Eastern Queen",' said Great Uncle Fletcher, his voice trembling slightly. 'A grand little engine. Well . . . well . . . well, eh?'

'Those were the days,' agreed Mr Denton, wringing Great Uncle Fletcher's hand violently. 'However, we must return to the present. My young friend here has put forward a most interesting scheme for the future use of the line. Although, I understand, there may be other people who also have a vested interest.'

'I did have,' agreed Red morosely. 'Me and my group were going to practise here, seeing as how there's nowhere in Aldport, but somebody's stolen all our gear.'

'Your gear,' said Mr Denton vaguely, 'I don't think I quite follow?'

'Oh Ellie!' said an anguished voice, from down the platform. 'Look what you've done now!'

'It *is* her,' said Great Uncle Fletcher and Andy in unison.

'It's Sue!' exclaimed Barny. 'But what's she doing here—and where is she?'

'Same place as she was before, I shouldn't wonder,' said Great Uncle Fletcher, 'when we had that last bit of bother and she got all ups-a-daisy about her "rights". What's more she *is* the littlest. . . .'

'Little enough to climb through the Booking Office window,' agreed Andy, nodding violently while an enormous grin spread across his freckled face as he turned to look at his cousin. Red stared back, went white, then pink and finally scarlet, his jaw chumping up and down.

'Perhaps,' Mr Denton said hopefully, 'somebody might explain?'

'No good asking me,' replied Uncle Ginger, 'I'm all at sea myself. We'd best just wait and listen, eh?'

'Eh,' agreed Mr Denton.

'She's stolen my gear,' roared Red, 'that's what she's done. Just wait till I get a hold of her. Just wait!'

He slammed out of the Booking Office and down the platform with such a fierce expression that the two newcomers to the Secret Railway were alarmed. The old hands took the situation more calmly.

'No need to fret,' said Great Uncle Fletcher soothingly. 'The little lass is quite safe where she is. There's not one of us here as can lay a hand on her till she chooses to come out and that's a fact. Got a lovely big bolt on the inside of the door it has.'

'Out of *where*?' asked Mr Denton trying hard to unravel all this extraordinary behaviour.

'The "Ladies Only" Waiting Room,' replied Barny. 'Oh good old Sue!'

'Come out, come out,' shouted Red, pushing and shoving with all his might. But it was a very solid door and it didn't budge a fraction.

'I shan't come out,' said a very dignified voice from the interior of the 'Ladies Only'. 'Go away, you're a nasty, horrid, rude boy and I don't like you. I'm not speaking to you because you want to make a mess of our Railway and we'd just got it all nice and neat again.'

'Have you got my instruments in there or haven't you?' demanded Red.

133

'Yes,' said Sue, quite forgetting that she wasn't speaking to him, 'all of them and I can stay here for days and days because I've got lots of food—so *there*!'

'But we've got an engagement to play at a dance tomorrow,' Red said, his voice changing from a roar to a quieter yet more desperate note. 'It's the first really good date we've ever been offered. We must have our instruments. We MUST.'

'Well you can't.'

'I—I—I'll kick the door down.'

The hands of Great Uncle Fletcher and Uncle Ginger Fletcher descended on Red's shoulders, Andy and Barny gripped hold of his shirt and Mr Denton said hurriedly, 'No, I think not. You'd need a battering-ram to break that door down, young man. I believe I'm starting to grasp the situation and if you want my advice you'll admit defeat and start to talk terms. Good morning, Miss Roberts. It's me you know, Mr Denton.'

'Good morning. Now, if you don't mind I'm going to have some breakfast.'

'She,' said Mr Denton, addressing the assembled company, 'has, to use a slang phrase, got us all over a barrel. Gentlemen, I think we should hold a conference.'

134

'Mister,' Red said desperately, 'I've got to get my instruments back. It's *important*.'

'Yes, yes, yes I do see that. Now let's see what we can work out by talking rather than by using force.'

Inside the 'Ladies Only' Sue was in far too much of a state to eat anything as her stomach was going round and round and she felt sick. Also she had just discovered that she had got another problem on her hands, a very messy one at that.

'Oh drat it,' she whispered and got down on her hands and knees and pressed her ear to the door to see if she could hear what was being said at the conference. But as it was taking place a little further down the platform she only caught a few words here and there.

'Guitar AND drums. . . .'

'A way of making use of the line. . . .'

'Sure the lad didn't mean any *real* harm, but there's not much for lads to do in these parts, no jobs neither. . . .'

'It is OUR secret railway. . . .'

'Other people taking it over—no!'

'Speaking as a Director of the Line. . . .'

'Would have to apply for a Light Railway Order. . . .'

'Know I shouldn't have done it, but there wasn't no other place to rehearse in. . . .'

'From the Secretary of State for the Environment I believe. . . .'

'But what about US?'

'Speaking as a Director of the Line. . . .'

'Could be a possible solution if it were run privately at the weekends. . . .'

Sue furrowed up her forehead, unable to make either head or tail of all this. She muttered, 'How they do go *on*! Oh Ellie, please come away from that drum, you've made enough mess already.'

'Tck, tck, tck, tck.'

'Lass,' said the rumbling voice of Great Uncle Fletcher so close to the keyhole that Sue almost fell over backwards. 'We've reached a compromise. Will you listen to it?'

'I might. Ellie, STOP that!'

'Will you trust me?'

Sue thought this over and then nodded, remembered that nobody could see her nodding and said, 'I trust YOU, Great Uncle Fletcher, so if you say it's OK, OK.'

'Good lass. Unbolt the door then.'

'It *is* unbolted. The lock's ever so shaky on this side and when Red said he was going to kick the door down I thought I'd better undo it because the plaster stuff is all crumbly. Really you could have pushed it open with one finger.'

Sue smiled at their surprised faces and Red opened and shut his mouth a couple of times and then, in spite of his own worries, he started to chuckle. Then the chuckle became a laugh and, as laughter is very catching, everybody else began to see the ridiculous side of the situation and they started to laugh too. The whole station echoed with the noise of people going, 'Ha, ha, HA', 'He, he HE', 'Ho, ho, HO,' 'Hum, hum, HUM' and Ellie came rushing out of the 'Ladies Only' and went scudding off down the platform to take refuge by the steps of the signal-box.

'Our terms are these,' said Great Uncle Fletcher huskily as he wiped his eyes. 'That young Red here gets back all his musical instruments and uses Marsh End of a Saturday for practising his songs and such. And—don't you frown at me, girl—him and his Group leaves the place as they finds it. Right?'

'Mm. EXACTLY as they find it, eh?'

'Exactly,' said Red. 'No more mess left about and that. We'll clear up after us, I promise. And I'm sorry about—well you know—and that. Only I got mad like, seeing all of you playing trains and enjoying it. Oh I dunno.'

'It's his red hair,' said Uncle Fletcher to no one in particular. 'He's up in a temper in a moment, but it doesn't last, like.'

'Yes, I see,' said Sue going rather pink. 'OK then. There is one thing I ought to tell you really, but never mind it now. Go on, Great Uncle Fletcher.'

'It's my turn actually,' said Mr Denton. 'As you know we've got rather a transport problem at my firm. If we open up a local factory how do people get to it to do their work? And how do we carry *what* they make back to the Midland depots?'

The assembled company shuffled their feet and tried to look as if they knew the right answer. They knew bits of it, but like the pieces in a jigsaw it didn't add up to a complete picture yet.

'What might—just might be a possible solution,' Mr Denton went on, 'would be to re-open this old railway line.'

Six mouths fell open and stayed like that for nearly a minute and then Andy said:

'But it's OUR railway.'

'No t'isn't,' said Great Uncle Fletcher. 'Shut down it maybe, but it still belongs to British Rail. And I never heard of 'em selling off their lines to anyone.'

'There's the Bluebell Line and. . . .' began Barny.

'Please,' Mr Denton raised his hand, 'please allow me to continue. I'm not too sure of the procedure, but I believe that if British Rail were willing to sell the land on which this line is laid. . . .'

'And the station—ouch,' said Sue subsiding as Barny nipped her arm. She retreated a couple of steps back into the 'Ladies Only', her mouth turning down at the corners, because all of a sudden it seemed as though whatever happened they were going to lose their secret railway after all.

'Sell the land,' Mr Denton began to speak more rapidly to try and stop any further interruptions, 'to GER, then I believe the firm could apply for a Light Railway Order from the Secretary of State for the Environment and. . . .'

'The who?' asked Red and was cuffed round the ear by his father.

'And if we *got* permission,' said Mr Denton, now gabbling his words together, 'we could re-open the line and run it ourselves. I mean GER would run it. There'd be a lot to go into, of course, and it might take a long time to work out so there's nothing to get too excited about *yet*.'

'I'm not excited at all,' said Andy dolefully. 'I

mean it'd be nice if the line is used again, but it wouldn't be anything to do with *us*.'

'If,' said Mr Denton, his voice becoming a kind of squeak, 'if it did work out all right and GER takes over Marsh End they will not be using it on Sundays. On Sundays—I beg your pardon Great Uncle, I mean Mr Fletcher, you wanted to say something?'

'I do. If I understands you correct, sir, seeing as how the Line'd be rightfully and properly maintained, we could run it Private on a Sunday. Right?'

'Right. But there are a great many problems to be tackled before we get anywhere near that situation. So please, please don't feel too optimistic as yet. It's only an idea in my head at the moment, you see.'

'It's a jolly good idea,' said Barny after another long pause. 'And we'll do everything we can to help you. In fact I'm starting to get some ideas already myself. . . .'

'Oh dear,' said Mr Denton. 'I mean, good, good. But first of all may I just ask, is it true that there's actually a 4–6–0T in that shed? May I see her?'

'You may indeed, sir,' said Great Uncle Fletcher, his jaw chomping up and down. 'Over here.'

'What ideas?' asked Andy, as Great Uncle

Fletcher, Uncle Ginger Fletcher and Mr Denton hurried off down the platform. 'And anyway I thought you wanted to go back to Birmingham, eh?'

'Not all that much,' said Barny, 'not now anyway. Well, first of all, supposing we get up one of those petition things. You know, you get people to sign it, because they think it's a smashing idea to get the line open again. . . .'

'I could go round the farms. . . .'

'And Sue and I could go round the town and—I say, Sue, that was a jolly good idea of yours to lock yourself in the "Ladies Only"—and then there are all the villages. We'll have to make out a list. . . .'

'I'll get my map. . . .'

'Yes, but look here,' said Sue, but she spoke to the empty air for the two boys with their heads close together, both of them talking at once, were hurrying off to the Booking Office. Sue sighed and then with a nervous jump realized that Red had slipped past her into the 'Ladies Only'.

'Oh dear,' whispered Sue and braced herself.

'Oi!' shouted a voice from the interior, 'Oi! You might have told me! What a *mess*!'

Sue put her head cautiously round the door and smiled nervously at Red whose face was once again the colour of his hair.

'I did try,' Sue said in a small voice. 'But Ellie had done it before I could stop her. And anyway, how was *I* to know that she'd lay an egg *inside* your guitar?'

Red tipped it up and a very scrambled egg slowly dripped out of it and splashed on to the floor.

'Look at it!' said Red, his voice getting angrier with each word.

There are times when it's wiser to run away from trouble and this definitely seemed to be one of them. The Third Director of the Line took two steps backwards and half a second later she was running as fast as she could for the safety of the engine shed.

Ellie stuck her head out from underneath the signal-box to see what all the fuss was about.

'Tck, tck, tck,' she said, ruffling her feathers. Her little black eyes shone wickedly as she looked up and down the now empty station. 'Tck, tck, TCK!'